# FRACTAL

## Bridge to the other side

## Gina Øster

Gina Øster

*FRACTAL – Bridge to the other side*

*Copyright © 2019 Gina Øster*
*Author: Gina Øster*
*Original title in Dutch: Fractal – Brug naar het Hiernamaals*
*English Translation: Gina Øster*
*Proofed by: Sebastiaan Kunst & Amanda Johnston*

*Photo Cover: Kellepics*

*ISBN: 978-10-9940-695-9*
*BISAC FIC009000*

# To Babou & Ollie

*No beginning, no end…*
*Merci!*

Gina Øster

# PROLOGUE

I can see them clearly now in their white coats, they are busy connecting machines to my body. After the extreme cold I have slipped out again. I'm suspended just below the ceiling. The EEG on the heart monitor shows a flat line, the blood is collected, the procedure is in full progress. Isabela is nervous, I try to reach out to her but she does not notice.

*I look in the laboratory; 3 people apparently dead under induced hypothermia, cooled down in specially insulated thermos bags to a temperature of just above freezing point. How many of us will return this time?*

*Suddenly I am drawn into a tunnel. Flashes of light pass me by, it is going faster and faster, it is breathtaking. As quickly as the tunnel starts so abruptly does it end. Then there is silence. A sensation of pure bliss and ecstasy takes hold of me. I am standing on the edge of a huge vortex. It is turning from the outside inwards like some kind of a spiral with an ever-higher speed. I am floating and yet I am not. This is the last stop. Freedom.*

*Slowly I start to move in the same rhythm as the vortex. A bright white light in the middle indicates two directions. One goes my way, the other to the unknown. There is no notion of time; I am as light as a feather. I am, but then differently. Bodyless, as free as a bird. A sense of immense peace enters my body. The white light is approaching, pure energy. White heavenly rays, so welcoming.*

*I see other appearances like myself. All on their way to the unknown. Some are being sent back, others continue their way. Strings are being tightened or let go ....*

* * *

# CHAPTER 1

## New York Times - 4 September 2036

Tomorrow, the representatives of the International Court of Ethics will come together at the Headquarters of the United Nations in New York, to evaluate the much-discussed ethical issue of the 'AfterLife Project'. The founders of the project, four of the world's greatest scientists, will be interrogated here in the next few days.

The 'AfterLife Project' (abbreviated ALP) was established by the company SITCO in 2030, with the aim of finding an answer to the question as to whether there is life after death. A team of scientists, physicians and specialists in the phenomenon of near-death experience have been working together since the launch of the project, and have finally found a way to make the journey to the hereafter. Their method consists of people experiencing a near-death experience by going near or even beyond the frontier of death and then returning to this earthly life.

The project is controversial. The candidates are placed in a laboratory under induced hypothermia. Their blood is replaced with a cold saline solution so that the temperature of their body decreases.

This method was called 'suspended animation' at the beginning of this century. At the time, it was applied to a very small number of patients who had suffered a cardiac arrest due to a severe trauma with a major loss of blood.

If body cells are cooled down they require less oxygen. Brain tissues that can normally only survive for a few minutes without oxygen will remain intact longer this way. This gives the surgeon more time to treat the trauma before the patient is warmed up again.

At the ALP, about a quarter of the candidates are healthy, the others are terminally ill or suffering from psychological problems such as depression or anxiety disorders. They end up in a life-threatening situation this way.

When scientists first applied this method to pigs just after the turn of the century, they maintained hypothermia of 10° C for a few seconds, followed by immediate warming up of the body. In the test phase on people that followed, the same temperature of 10° C was maintained but for a slightly longer time. The candidates were connected to a heart-lung machine immediately after cooling down so that the brain would quickly be supplied with oxygen. According to the statistics, this method was applied at the time to a total of 162 patients, more than half of whom died…

The ALP started with hypothermia of 10° C. At a later stage, they dropped the temperature to just above freezing point. The controversy is that they keep the candidates in this condition for an increasingly longer period of time before they connect them to the heart-lung machine. This means a rising risk of complications, possibly leading to death.

But that is not all. The ALP wants to go even further, by cooling down the bodies in an even more radical way. They want to use a method called 'brain vitrification', in which brain tissues are cooled down to -124° C. According to various sources there is a considerable danger of brain injury or even of never waking up again...

To obtain a statistically plausible result for their research, the ALP requires a great many candidates. The number of people who have participated since the start of the actual survey in June last year is over 2,700. According to our sources, more than 400 died. Although this concerns people who volunteered, it does raise the question: is this ethically acceptable?

Thanks to social media, the ALP has now hundreds of thousands of followers worldwide. In the last quarter, it even raised an additional 63 million dollars for its research. The remarkable results and the expected imminent breakthrough have even led to a waiting list of volunteers to participate in the programme.

However, the project also meets with fierce opposition, especially from religious communities. It is through them in particular, through the spiritual leaders of the International Christian Society and of the Roman Catholic Church, that this case has been presented to the Court of Ethics with the question as to whether this kind of research is permitted in our society or if it should be prohibited.

The International Court of Ethics of the United Nations was established in 2025 after the worldwide scandal regarding failed nanochip implants in demented elderly people. It has dealt with some major issues over the past few years, such as the SpaceOne affair, the company that in 2033, after several unsuccessful attempts, finally managed to put the first human being on planet Mars.

The Council consists of five judges, chosen by the joint Member States. It is chaired by Antoni Riberi from Switzerland, and will ultimately decide whether the ALP should stop their research or if they can go ahead.

\* \* \*

"The idea that the order and
the precision of the universe
in all its innumerable aspects would
be the result of a blind coincidence,
is as credible as if after the
explosion of a printing press
all the characters would fall on
the ground in the order of a dictionary."

Albert Einstein

"In the beginning there was nothing,
which exploded"

Terry Pratchett

"Nothing cannot exist forever"

Stephen Hawking

# CHAPTER 2

## 5 September 2036

New York - International Court of Ethics
Court hearing of the AfterLife Project

Members of the Board :

1. Chairman Prof Antoni Riberi – Switzerland
2. Prof Yannis Cohn – United States
3. Prof Rosa Bernstein – Germany
4. Prof Hanna Linstrøm – Denmark
5. Prof Jon Bennett – United Kingdom

Defendants:

1. Prof Jack Brigance – Scientist at SITCO (Scientific Institute of Technology of Colorado), United States
2. Prof Robert Greene – Cardiologist and Traumatologist at the University General Hospital in Boston, United States
3. Prof Kurt Susskind – Scientist at SITCO (Scientific Institute of Technology of Colorado), United States

4. Prof Léon Tautou – Neurologist and Philosopher at the Centre Hospitalier Universitaire in Lausanne, Switzerland

## Transcription - Morning of Day 1

Speakers:    Antoni Riberi – Chairman of the Board
             Jack Brigance – Defendant

A. Riberi: 'Ladies and gentlemen, as President of the International Court of Ethics, I would like to welcome you to this closed hearing. At the end of this hearing, the Board will decide whether the AfterLife Project, from now on abbreviated to ALP, must be prohibited, and if those present should be prosecuted, or if the project may continue. During this hearing, all judges will be able to question the defendants.'

'We obviously ask all who are present in this room for total discretion; there should not be any contact with the press until after the verdict.'

'Mr Brigance, since you are the director of the ALP, we will start with you. Please explain why you and your colleagues decided to start this project.'

J. Brigance: 'Dear members of the Board, the answer to this question is threefold.'

'Firstly, everyone has sometimes wondered if there is life after death. What happens when we die? Most of us would like to know if there is some sort of life after death, and if so, what it looks like. Every religious movement has its own ideas but nobody knows if there is actually something.'

'There has been some great technological progress in the scientific and medical world in the past decades. We have learned a great deal about the origin of the universe, about black holes, about atoms and the even smaller elementary particles; but also about the human body, about brain diseases and about the near-death experience.'

'Scientists, medical specialists, philosophers and specialists in near-death experience are often focused only on their own fields. By combining their knowledge, we have created the possibility of looking further and deeper. We have now come to the point where it is possible to send the first person to the afterlife and let him return back safely to earth.'

'Secondly, an answer to the question as to whether there is life after death could take away the fear that is felt by many of us. How many people are afraid of death and live their entire lives in fear? Many religions hold their communities together by preaching about the hereafter, about heaven and hell, about the penance that needs to be done if strict rules are not followed here on earth. If we have a clear picture of what comes after death, life on earth will be lived with less anxiety and more happiness.'

'And thirdly, this might create the possibility of placing all religions under one name, a universal religion as it were. After all, people will then know what is coming, where we are going, whether there is a God or not. Most wars are caused by religious beliefs. If we gain more certainty about what happens after death, there are likely to be fewer religious conflicts, and ultimately therefore fewer wars.'

A. Riberi: 'Mr Brigance, I think that we would all be happy to live a life without fear and to find more peace on earth. You sketch a beautiful but rather idealistic utopia here.'

'Before going any further I would like to remind you and your colleagues that we are here to judge the way in which you seek answers to the question of whether there is life after death, and not the fact that you are looking for answers. This is contrary to the rumours on social media that we have already come to a verdict under pressure from various religious communities.'

J. Brigance: 'Sir, we will give you a full explanation of our research. We will show you that the benefits by far outweigh the risks and that promising results have already been achieved.'

A. Riberi: 'Very well, Mr Brigance, please proceed.'

J. Brigance: 'Your Honour, we will start by giving you an overview of what has happened in our respective disciplines during the past few decades. My colleague Kurt Susskind and I will give you a detailed outline on physics, followed by our colleague Léon Tautou, who will give you information on near-death experiences. After this, we will collate all this information and, together with our colleague Robert Greene, we will give you a deep insight into our research.'

A. Riberi: 'You have the floor, Mr Brigance, go ahead.'

J. Brigance: 'As far as physics is concerned, you probably know that there are two theories, one relates to the largest, the universe; the other is about the smallest, atoms and the even smaller quantum particles.'

'I will start by giving you an overview of the theory of the largest. My colleague Kurt will then follow with the theory about the smallest. The latter is quite complicated and will therefore be dealt with more broadly. Do not hesitate to interrupt us and ask questions; it is very important that you understand all the theories. It has become clear from our research that the world of the smallest, the quantum world, and near-death experiences cannot be viewed separately from each other.'

A. Riberi: 'Understood, please continue.'

J. Brigance: 'Right, let me start with a little explanation about the origin of the universe:

'A few years ago, it became clear that the universe indeed originated after a 'big bang', a very small point of pure energy that exploded. This energy had such tremendous power that, in a very short time it created all the mass and energy in the now existing 200 billion galaxies, and at the same time shaped all the laws of nature and natural forces that are known today.'

A. Riberi: 'To which natural forces do you refer, Mr Brigance?'

J. Brigance: 'As far as we know, there are four natural forces. The gravitational force which holds together the universe and which is found at the level of the largest; and the electromagnetic force, the strong nuclear force and the weak nuclear force which are found at the level of subatomic particles, which will be discussed later by my colleague Kurt.'

'We are all familiar with gravitational force. For example, if we drop an object from our hands, the gravity of the earth will attract it and make it fall to the ground. In addition, it ensures, for example, that the moon rotates around the earth and does not, as it were, 'fly straight ahead'.'

'If gravity had been very different, the universe would not look like it does now. Computers have calculated that, with very weak gravity, there would be nothing at all; all matter would fly so fast that galaxies could never be formed. Equally, very strong gravity would not work either, everything would clump together in one big black hole because black holes have the highest gravity in the universe.'

A. Riberi: 'Mr Brigance, although most of us have probably heard about black holes, you might want to elaborate on this?'

J. Brigance: 'Your Honour, it is indeed important that you understand this properly. For our research, four universal phenomena turned out to be very important: black holes, wormholes, dark matter and dark energy. We will address them all here.'

'A black hole is formed after the explosion of a very large star, called a supernova. We have one in our own milky way, Sagittarius

A. When such a star comes to the end of its life, it grows and grows until it eventually explodes. Because of the extreme gravity in the centre the core implodes (it collapses), and continues as a black hole.

'A black hole owes its name to two things: firstly, everything of matter and gas that is present in its surroundings, such as stars and planets, disappears into it, as if it were falling into a hole. Secondly, as light is also swallowed, everything in the surroundings will become dark (black).'

'You can visualise a black hole by thinking of a funnel. It is wide at the top and narrow at the bottom, like a spout. When a pellet is set in motion at the top of the funnel, it will spiral from top to bottom with increasing speed. This also applies to black holes. Stars near a black hole rotate faster and faster until they are swallowed up and are no longer visible.'

'The wide top edge of a black hole is called the event horizon. Light can still escape from the force of gravity at this point. However, everything that goes beyond this edge is swallowed up and cannot escape.'

'The narrow spout on the other side of the black hole ends in a very small point, called singularity. This corresponds to the smallest particles in the quantum world.'

'So, on one side there is a wide edge where whole galaxies with a span of thousands of light years are swallowed up, and on the other hand it all disappears in a very small point that is smaller than a grain of sand. A combination that is very difficult for us to imagine, and yet that is how it is....'

'Since a black hole is invisible, it was impossible until recently to know what happened to the matter once it crossed the horizon. Many scientists assumed that everything that disappears into a black hole would be pulled apart like spaghetti because the gravity here is so incredibly strong that it outweighs the speed of light. However, we have discovered that something very different happens.'

A. Riberi: 'Wait a moment Mr Brigance. Your story is not entirely clear. What do you mean by 'being pulled apart like spaghetti because the strong gravity outweighs the speed of light?''

J. Brigance: 'Do you know what is meant by the speed of light?'

A. Riberi: 'Yes, but please explain again.'

J. Brigance: 'The speed of light is the highest speed that exists in the universe. Nothing can move faster. Light moves at about 300,000 km per second. This is so incredibly fast that we cannot even imagine it.'

'For example, light moves more than seven times around the earth in less than one second and it covers the distance to the moon in just over a second.'

'Since the distances to other stars and galaxies are so gigantic, another kind of measurement is used at the universal level, called light years.'

'So, if we consider that the speed of light is 300,000 km per second, then a light year is no less than 9.5 trillion kilometres.'

A. Riberi: "Is it not true that everything we see in the starry sky actually represents a picture of the past?'

J. Brigance: 'Yes indeed. All the stars are so far away that the light dots we see have left their origin many years ago before arriving at our planet. For example, the nearest star Proxima Centauri is 4.3 light years away from the earth. This means that, when we see Proxima Centauri, we see the light dots that were radiated more than four years ago. It could very well be that this star looks very different now or perhaps no longer exists! This phenomenon is called optical illusion.'

'Now, to answer your earlier question: spaghettification is the vertical stretching and horizontal compression of objects into long and thin shapes (rather like spaghetti) in the very strong gravitational field of a black hole. The gravitational force is so strong that no object can resist it, not even light.'

A. Riberi: 'Okay, understood.'

J. Brigance: 'Good, now to go back to the black holes and the funnels, you must know that all particles in the universe have an associated antiparticle. Their properties are exactly the opposite, that is why they are also called 'mirror images of particles'. In physics, these particles and anti-particles are also known as matter and antimatter. Antimatter is invisible. When two particles collide with each other (annihilate), they explode into energy, and become visible in the form of a very dense light or another form of radiation (X-rays or gamma-rays for example).'

A. Riberi: 'Do you mean these mysterious flashes of light that are sometimes detected by telescopes?'

J. Brigance: 'Yes exactly. Scientists used to think that these mysterious flashes of light were pulsars (a pulsar is a collapsed star that emits radiation at the end of its life). But when it became clear that pulsars are continuously transmitting radiation, and that these light flashes only emit for a very short time period, it was clear that the source had to originate somewhere else.'

'Our research has shown that this source can be found in the surroundings of the black hole. As I just said, each particle has an antiparticle. A black hole also has a counterpart: a white hole. When they encounter each other, a short explosion occurs that causes a flash of light.'

A. Riberi: 'A white hole? I have not heard of that before. What is that exactly?'

J. Brigance: 'A white hole can be visualised as a reverse funnel. On the wide edge (event horizon), it has a negative gravity. In other words, it pushes away from itself, like two positive magnets; a kind of anti-electromagnetic force.'

'In short, this means that everything first disappears into the black hole because of its major gravity, then, once it reaches the narrow end of the funnel it meets its counterpart, the white hole. There is a collision between the two; an explosion, after which the matter is spat out again through the negative gravity force of the white hole. The narrow point in the middle where matter and antimatter meet forms the passage between the black and white hole.'

A. Riberi: 'Okay, understood.'

J. Brigance: 'Right. I spoke to you about the big bang earlier on. To continue on this subject, several colleagues are currently finalising the evidence that our big bang was one of many, and that other big bangs are taking place elsewhere, even now at this very moment, which means that there would be multiple universes; the so-called multiverse.'

A. Riberi: 'I indeed read something about this subject recently. What is this multiverse according to you?'

J. Brigance: 'The universe is finite without having an edge or border. If you think of a sphere or a globe (like the earth, for example), we can move across the surface without ever encountering a boundary. Yet it is finite in size. For example, if you wanted to paint the entire sphere in green, you would not need an infinite amount of paint.'

'Now imagine this sphere as an air bubble that is becoming larger and larger, expanding further and further. We live on the surface of that gigantic bubble, like flies stuck on adhesive paper. This air bubble is located in a sea with other air bubbles, which together form

- like some kind of a bubble bath - the multiverse. From time to time those bubbles collide, which causes a new big bang.'

A. Riberi: 'The question of course is whether this multiverse exists or whether it is just a philosophical theory.'

'I suggest that we first have a short break and that we resume in half an hour. In the opposite room you can find coffee, tea and soft drinks.'

* * *

# CHAPTER 3

*In SITCO's laboratory - Colorado*

*8 weeks earlier...*

It is hot in the little room, the air conditioning is running at full power. Next to me are two older gentlemen and two young women. In front of us is a lady in a wheelchair. Three speakers are standing next to a big presentation screen which shows the letters ALP. The speakers are certainly competent. Two highly educated scientists talk about black holes and quantum strings. The third person, a woman, talks about the near-death experience. For most of us this is a difficult subject, too theoretical, too incomprehensible.

Silence in the room. Everybody is listening. They say that already more than 2,700 volunteers have preceded us. Not everybody has come back alive…

They want to go further into the black hole. To be the first to send a human being to the hereafter and let him return safely back to earth. With the new method, this should work. They are looking for benevolent pioneers. We are the chosen ones.

We are being told that in the coming weeks we will first undergo a 'normal' near-death experience, via the old method. Then we will be prepared for the ultimate trip. Do we still want to participate after this explanation? Nobody hesitates. We are all here with a specific purpose.

I already knew at an early age that I was different. When I was about 13 years old, I already wondered why it was me who was in this body. That a new person could be created through some joyful intimate interplay between two adults I could understand, but where did my 'I' come from? It could not be that in every single one of my father's millions of spermatozoids a soul and consciousness exist or that the soul and consciousness suddenly come to life in my mother's ovaries, could it? Was my thinking self, with all its feelings and emotions, an illusion created by the outside world, and was my other, observing self, perhaps part of something far bigger?

At the beginning of the year, I saw the announcement of the ALP; gigantic! An opportunity to look behind the scenes of the universe. To find answers to important existential life questions, such as who or what is God really? Is it an anthropomorphic figure, an old man with a beard, as many people imagine it, or is it a higher power of energy? Is the universe controlled by a computer program or are the old mythical texts correct in saying that it is the extra-terrestrial Annunaki who created man?

Are there any risks involved in this research? Yes. Can it go wrong during the procedure? Yes. Do I want to die? No. Why am I participating? The intense hunger for knowledge.

Risks are everywhere. The ALP procedure seems reliable ...., well, at least the procedure that has been applied so far. And as the sayings go: 'Where there is a will there is a way', and 'Wonders never cease'. I believe that, if you want to move forward in science and find answers to complex questions, you must dare to take certain risks ...

\* \* \*

"Look deep into nature
and you will understand everything better"

Albert Einstein

"Man lives on nature – means that nature is his body,
with which he must remain in continuous
interchange if he is not to die.
That man's physical and spiritual life is linked to nature
means simply that nature is linked to itself,
for man is part of nature"

Karl Marx

"If we change the way we look at things,
the things we look at will change"

Wayne Dyer

# CHAPTER 4

## 5 September 2036

New York - International Court of Ethics
Court hearing of the AfterLife Project

Transcription - Morning of Day 1 - continued

Speakers:    Antoni Riberi – Chairman of the Board
             Jack Brigance – Defendant

A. Riberi: 'Welcome back ladies and gentlemen.'

'Mr Brigance, before the break you were talking about matter and antimatter. If antimatter exists, does that mean that there is also something like an anti-universe?'

J. Brigance: 'That is a good question. We expect that it indeed exists. A universe that collides with an anti-universe causes an explosion, just as matter and antimatter do when they encounter each other. How this works exactly is not entirely clear because we have not yet been able to look outside the universe. What we do know is that there are several dimensions. Dimensions that we as human beings cannot experience because they are at a level in space we cannot reach with our senses. Later on, we will explain to you what happens to our candidates when they are brought under induced hypothermia. The other dimension they experience could indeed be seen as another universe, or, why not, as an anti-universe.'

A. Riberi: 'Okay. Please continue.'

J. Brigance: 'I would like to go back to the big bang once again.'

A. Riberi: 'Very well, please proceed.'

J. Brigance: 'After the first cooling down, the energy of the explosion was converted into very small subatomic particles. That was the first matter in the universe. About three minutes later, the first elements hydrogen, helium and lithium were formed; the building blocks of everything that exists around us. In this short time of three minutes, the universe extended from a small dot to a huge span of several light years.'

A. Riberi: 'Mr Brigance, how do we know exactly when the big bang took place?'

J. Brigance: 'The universe came into existence about 13.7 billion years ago. We know this because we can look back in time with our advanced telescopes. The Hubble telescope showed at the beginning of this century, that galaxies move away from us at great speed. Matter that moves away from us must have been together at one point originally; this is just a matter of logical reasoning. By measuring the speed of the expansion, you can calculate how old the universe is.'

A. Riberi: 'And what was there before the big bang?'

J. Brigance: 'With the word 'before', you talk about a timeline. However, time only started after the big bang. The question 'what was there before the big bang?' can therefore only be answered with 'there was nothing because there was not yet any time.'

A. Riberi: 'I understand. You just spoke about the expansion of the universe. What exactly do you mean by that?'

J. Brigance: 'I just gave you the example of a bubble that gets bigger and bigger. You could also compare it to a balloon. Imagine you paint little stars on the balloon with a marker. When you blow up the balloon, more space is created between the stars. So, it is not the stars that move away from each other, but rather that more space is being formed between them.'

A. Riberi: 'Okay, that makes sense. Please continue.'

J. Brigance: 'I would like to take you on a little trip back in history to illustrate what we know about how the universe operates.'

A. Riberi: 'We are listening.'

J. Brigance: 'As you probably know, Copernicus introduced his mathematical theory in the 15th and 16th century, explaining that the sun is the centre of the solar system and that the planets rotate around it. This was confirmed and published by the inventor of the telescope, Galileo Galilei (16th and 17th century).'

'His publication, incidentally, caused a conflict with the Roman Catholic Church, since he argued against their view that the earth was the centre of the universe. Because of this, Galileo had to appear twice before the Inquisition and was eventually considered a heretic. For centuries, some of his works were on the list of books that Catholics were not allowed to read. It was only in 1992 (no kidding!) that the Pope acknowledged the Catholic Church had wrongly condemned Galileo.'

'This is just an aside, to give you an example of conflictual behaviour between church and individual if the individual does not live according to the norms and values prescribed by the church (and thus by religion).'

'Isaac Newton followed with his theory of gravity in the 17th and 18th century, followed by Albert Einstein in the 19th and 20th century, with his theory of relativity that describes gravity and the universe in terms of the curving of space-time.'

'Einstein's theory is important for our research as we talk a lot about energy. His famous equation is, as you know, $E = mc^2$. The E stands for energy, m stands for mass, and $c^2$ for the speed of light squared. Put very simply, this equation says that mass (matter) and energy are equivalent. They are two forms of the same: energy is liberated matter, and matter is potential energy. Because $c^2$ is really a gigantic number, the equation actually says that there is an enormous amount of energy (and I mean a really enormous amount of energy) trapped in every piece of matter.'

A. Riberi: 'This is especially evident in quantum mechanics isn't it?'

J. Brigance: 'The energy of all matter can indeed be traced back to nano or quantum level, in atoms and even smaller particles. My colleague Kurt Susskind will tell you more about this later.'

A. Riberi: 'What else can you tell us about Einstein's space-time?'

J. Brigance: 'We naturally regard space and time as entirely separate concepts. That is logical because we can freely move through space, but the movement in time seems unchangeable.'
    'Einstein thought differently. With his theory of relativity, he created a fourth dimension out of space and time, the so-called 'space-time' continuum. According to him, these two could not be seen separately.'

A. Riberi: 'Can you explain further please?'

J. Brigance: 'Of course. We all know the three axes that we use to orient ourselves in space: forward-backward, left-right and up-down. According to Einstein, time is a fourth axis: from past to future (going from left to right on a graphical chart).'

A. Riberi: 'I understand that. Space-time also has some weird properties doesn't it?'

J. Brigance: 'True. The space-time continuum is also something very strange. For example, time runs more slowly as you move, but faster when you are on top of a mountain, and it stops at the event horizon of a black hole. It is admirable that Einstein already suggested this more than a hundred years ago because, according to our research, it is indeed true that time stops at the event horizon of a black hole.'

A. Riberi: 'That is indeed quite remarkable.'

J. Brigance: Einstein also said that black holes might have unusual properties. For example, the central point could form a bridge to another universe, the so called wormhole, or Einstein-Rosen bridge....'

A. Riberi: 'Mr Brigance, you are talking about black holes, white holes and now about wormholes; that is a lot of holes in the universe!'
'In science fiction films, they often talk about these wormholes. If I am right, this means that one can travel from one universe to another in a few seconds, is that right?'

J. Brigance: 'Yes indeed, wormholes are shortcuts through time and space. One could, for example, travel from one galaxy to another, or to the past or future; it can go every which way. The idea behind a wormhole is that it reduces the distance between two points in space and time.'

A. Riberi: 'Aha, and why is it called a wormhole?'

J. Brigance: 'A wormhole derives its name from the worm that digs through an apple. Suppose that the outside of the universe is the skin of an apple and the worm wants to go from one side to the other, then if it remains on the skin, the shortest distance is half the circumference of the apple. But if the worm digs a hole straight through the apple, the distance is considerably less, namely the diameter of the apple. Another example: take the letter U and rotate it 90° so that the long legs are placed horizontally above each other. Then draw a vertical line from the upper leg to the lower leg, this is the wormhole. Without this vertical line you would have to go from top to bottom through the big bend. While you could get from A to B much faster via the vertical line. In fact, it is a kind of bridge between two points.'

A. Riberi: 'Okay, understood.'

J. Brigance: 'As I said before, it is not possible to travel faster than the speed of light, so if you travel via the normal 'route', you can never go faster than 300,000 km per second. Through the wormhole it is possible to travel faster, because you are taking a shortcut. The universe is so enormous that it would be impossible to travel from one side to the other without wormholes; the distances would simply be too great.'

'To give you an idea: the perceptible part of the universe is 45 billion lightyears around us. The fastest spacecraft travels at about 250,000 km per hour. Quite quickly, you will think, but it is only 2.3% of the speed of light! And with this speed it would take 75,000 years to reach the nearest star Proxima Centauri!'

'Anyway, as I just said, in our research it has become clear that wormholes do indeed exist. We will come back to this later on.'

A. Riberi: 'We cannot wait to hear more about your discoveries, Mr Brigance! Are you finished or are there any other things you wish to share with us?'

J. Brigance: 'I have nearly finished and would just like to tell you something more about dark matter and dark energy if I may.'

A. Riberi: 'Please go ahead.'

J. Brigance: 'We can only observe 4% of the universe, including the stars and planets. The remainder consists of dark matter (28%) and dark energy (68%). Both are called dark because they are invisible.'

'Dark matter is known to hold galaxies together. Without this matter, galaxies would disintegrate according to the laws of physics because there is not enough gravity within the system to hold this rotating mass together.'

'Dark energy is actually even more mysterious. The only thing science knew until recently is that it is responsible for accelerating the expansion of the universe.'

'In recent months we have made a few very interesting discoveries about what this energy exactly means. But first I would like to give the floor to my colleague Kurt Susskind, who will give you a detailed explanation about physics at the smallest level: quantum mechanics.'

A. Riberi: 'Thank you very much Mr Brigance. I hereby suspend the hearing until after lunch. As mentioned earlier, there should not be any contact with the press. You are requested to be back in this room again at 14.00 hours.'

\* \* \*

# CHAPTER 5

*In SITCO's laboratory - Colorado*

*8 weeks earlier...*

The laboratory is huge. In the middle is a dividing wall, and behind it a gigantic opening in a rock. Inside the rock, there are four custom-made freezers standing against a wall. Next to it, is every possible item of medical equipment. The head of the medical staff Isabela informs us of what is going to happen in the coming weeks. We are split into two groups. The older gentlemen and the lady in the wheelchair together, and we, the slightly younger ones, in the other group. For each test, one or more persons from each group will be brought to a state of near-death for a varying number of minutes.

The procedure asks a lot of the body. Recovery takes at least four weeks. The ultimate journey will take place in about three months.

At one end of the laboratory is a door with a specially disinfected isolation room behind it: again, split into two parts, one part in the rock, the other outside. Both parts have a minimally furnished living room with two sleeping areas. No windows. Our bivouac for the coming time. No physical contact with the outside world during the entire period. Only contact with doctors in specially equipped suits. All possible risks of contamination are minimised. We depend on one another.


Our group is varied. The youngest, the South African paediatrician Nathalie, thinks that everything is predestined and that we have no influence on the date of our death. All is going as it should go and it could not be any different. So, if she dies in the coming months during one of the tests, she would have died elsewhere anyway, even if she had not participated in the programme.

The sporty Solenn from France is a biologist and is currently researching life in Antarctica. She wants to know whether the earthly cruelty of man changes in the goodness of heaven after death.

And then there is me, a Spanish half-breed who thinks that everything around us is just one big bundle of energy, and who is participating mainly out of pure curiosity.

We are told that, during the procedure, all the blood will be removed from our bodies, creating a situation of apparent death. This is the moment when the near-death experience should be taking place. We will be kept cool for a certain time after which we will be connected to the heart-lung machine and warmed up again.

That is if all goes well ....


\* \* \*

"The purpose of all experience is to
discover the true value of things"

Krishnamurti

"There is no unique
picture of reality"

Stephen Hawking

"The most beautiful we can experience
is the mysterious;
It is the source of all true
art and science"

Albert Einstein

# CHAPTER 6

## 5 September 2036

New York - International Court of Ethics

Court hearing of the AfterLife Project

Transcription - Afternoon of Day 1

Speakers:     Antoni Riberi – Chairman of the Board
              Kurt Susskind – Defendant

A. Riberi: 'Welcome back everyone. As you have probably noticed, there is a large crowd of people outside. You will therefore be requested to stay inside the building as of now. At the end of the afternoon, a special escort will take you to your accommodation through the back of the building.'

'The floor is yours Mr Susskind.'

K. Susskind: 'Dear members of the Board. As quantum mechanics is very complex, I will give you a more extensive explanation. And do not worry if you do not quite understand it; most of us physicists have great difficulty understanding how it works! I will give examples to make it all a bit more comprehensible.'

A. Riberi: 'That seems like a good idea.'

K. Susskind: 'As you know, the quantum theory describes the world of the smallest. Part of this world can be found for example in nanotechnology, of which we have heard quite a lot in the medical field these past decades.'

'In the world of the smallest, there are three fundamental forces: electromagnetism, and strong and weak nuclear forces. Without going into too much detail, we can say that the electromagnetic force is the source of things such as electricity and light, radio waves, microwaves and X-rays. The way we live in this day and age, with computers, smartphones, washing machines, TV, cars et cetera, would not have been possible without electromagnetic force.'

'The strong nuclear force is the strongest force of all. It keeps atomic nuclei together.'

'The weak nuclear force is responsible for the radioactive decay of certain nuclei.'

A. Riberi: 'You say that the strong nuclear force is the strongest force in the universe, but I thought that was gravity?'

K. Susskind: 'That may indeed seem to be the case because gravity shows such strong power at a black hole, but in fact it is the weakest force of all.'

A. Riberi: 'Right, please continue.'

K. Susskind: 'Before going further into the details of quantum mechanics, it may be useful if I first explain what atoms are, since these are the small particles that we will be talking about quite a lot in the coming days.'

A. Riberi: 'I think that we all have an idea of what atoms are but please go ahead.'

K. Susskind: 'Atoms are so small that they cannot even be seen with a microscope. The word atom comes from the Greek word a-tomos and literally means 'indivisible'. It is the smallest building block of chemical elements such as gold, iron, oxygen and nitrogen. We know that there are 118 of these kinds of elements on earth. We also know that everything we can see in the universe also consists of these same elements. For example, we know that the moon consists of various elements including hydrogen and iron; that Mars contains a lot of iron which, combined with oxygen, gives its famous rust-red colour, and that our sun mainly consists of hydrogen and helium (and is actually no more than a large sphere of hot gas).'

'Everything comes back to these 118 elements in the universe and on earth. We ourselves and everything around us, such as cars, stones, trees and flowers, also consist of these same elements. Our body, for example, consists mainly of hydrogen, oxygen, carbon and nitrogen, with a little bit of phosphorus and calcium.'

A. Riberi: 'Mr Susskind, I have heard that 'temperature', where we think of heat and cold, is actually nothing more than a number of colliding atoms, is that true?'

K. Susskind: 'Yes Sir, that's right. Billions of atoms constantly collide with each other, which produces a lot of energy and therefore heat. It gets warmer in the summer because sunlight activates atoms. This increases the degree to which they collide. When you feel the warmth of the sun on your back on a summer's day, you are actually feeling excited atoms! The higher you climb, the fewer molecules and atoms there are and therefore the fewer collisions, or the colder it becomes.'

A. Riberi: 'Interesting. Please continue.'

K. Susskind: 'Well, we can analyse an atom even further. Most atoms have three different subatomic particles inside them: protons, neutrons, and electrons. The protons and neutrons are packed together into the centre of the atom (which is called the nucleus) and the electrons, which are very much smaller, circle around it.'

'But most of an atom is just empty space.'

'And the latter is actually quite bizarre, because you could then say that all matter around us, and we ourselves, are actually mainly empty. To give you an example: if we would enlarge an atom thirty million times, let's say to the size of a football field, the nucleus would be about the size of a tomato seed. The electrons that circle around it would be even smaller, about the size of a grain of sand. For the rest, the entire football field would just be empty ... '

'So, everything that we see around us, such as a couch, a car, a tree, et cetera, is in fact no more than an illusion because everything is actually largely empty. It is a funny world, the world of the smallest!

A. Riberi: 'I have heard that people also compare atoms to Lego bricks?'

K. Susskind: 'You can indeed compare atoms to Lego bricks. They are solid and never break. When atoms that are stuck together get separated (by death for example), they will end up with other atoms to form something else. They never get lost and never disappear. The same applies to Lego bricks, one day you can make a house and the next day a castle, they remain solid unbreakable parts.'

A. Riberi: 'Understood. Please continue.'

K. Susskind: 'Right, now, in order to return to quantum mechanics, a group of scientists, led by the Danish physicist Niels Bohr, discovered in the early twentieth century that probability and uncertainty play a major role at the quantum level, whereas, according to his contemporary Einstein, everything in the big world, or in the universe, is orderly and predictable. According to Bohr, the world of the smallest is chaotic and unpredictable. Subatomic particles do not appear to be solid objects, but vibrating energy packages that sometimes behave like waves and sometimes like particles.'

A. Riberi: 'What do you mean by that?'

K. Susskind: 'That energy packages sometimes behave like waves and sometimes like particles?'

A. Riberi: 'Yes.'

K. Susskind: 'Well, a wave is something that wobbles in space and time. A large number of vibrating energy packages combined are called a wave. They stretch out over a certain distance. If one of these packages becomes a piece of solid matter, then it is called a particle.'

A. Riberi: 'And when is that?'

K. Susskind: 'According to the laws of quantum mechanics, a particle is located in an exact location once it has been observed by a spectator at that location. Until that time it remains a wave. If, for example, there are one thousand possibilities, they could all happen until they are observed. As soon as observation takes place, only one option remains out of the thousand possibilities. That is why we say that the particle can be 'anywhere and nowhere' at the same time, it depends on when and where observation takes place.'

'This theory about chance and uncertainty was something Einstein could scarcely believe. His famous statement was: 'God does not play dice'. In the world as we know it, we cannot walk through a door of steel, for example, while according to the laws of quantum mechanics there should be this possibility; after all, everything is possible.'

A. Riberi: 'Mr Susskind, if a particle is only in a certain position after it has been observed at that location, then my question is: what kind of reality would exist when no observation takes place? Then nothing really exists, does it?'

K. Susskind: 'That is a very good question Sir. Einstein also noted in his time that according to this theory it should be the case that, if he looks up to the sky at night and sees the moon, the moon would not exist as soon as he turned around again because there is no one who is observing the moon.'

'We call this the uncertainty principle, or the Copenhagen Interpretation of Heisenberg and Bohr. They said (and with them many others) that the world does not exist at the moment that one does not look. These physicists claim that an observation creates a personal world out of an infinite number of possibilities. And they are not really wrong. Just look at someone under hypnosis. If you tell a hypnotised person that everyone present in the room is bald, then they actually see that everyone is bald. How is this possible? Well, one of the thousands of possibilities according to quantum mechanics is that all heads are bald. In order to actually observe this, the person in question hears just before the observation under hypnosis that all heads are bald. As soon as they open their eyes and actually do the observation, this is the truth their brain tells them. Or another example: if someone is told under hypnosis that they are being touched with a very hot object while in reality this is only a pencil, their body will create a blister on the skin.'

'So, in other words, consciousness is 'instructed' by hypnosis how it will perceive the environment, and how reality will be experienced.'

A. Riberi: 'You mean that what the individual receives and what is perceived does not necessarily have to match with reality?'

K. Susskind: 'Exactly. We assume that we all see the world in the same way all the time, that everyone sees the same colours, that light is equally clear to everyone, that temperature is just as fresh, that voices are equally shrill. However, the opposite is closer to the truth. How we perceive the world around us varies enormously for each individual. Everyone experiences a colour or a shape in a different way.'

A. Riberi: 'Okay, understood, please continue.'

K. Susskind: 'In addition to the uncertainty principle about where the particle is located, another characteristic of the quantum mechanics is that particles influence each other while they are very far apart.'

'In 1925, Bohr stated that particles, even if they are separated by very significant distances, can immediately 'know' what the other particle is doing at that same moment. We could see this as some sort of quantum voodoo. If, for example, in our normal classical world we take a white and a blue marble and we look at the white one, we would believe that it was white before we looked. That is the normal course of events. Einstein thought so too. But, if we take two quantum marbles, also a white one and a blue one, then the colours will mix as soon as we bring them together. They even mix in such a way that you can no longer say which of those marbles is blue and which is white. We only know that there is a blue one and a white one. If we were to disassemble them, the mixture of both colours would remain the same. This is called entanglement.'

'And now comes the weird part. If we now look at one of those marbles and thus force the marble to choose colour, it will turn either white or blue. And.... if it turns white, then the other becomes instantaneously, that is to say at exactly the same moment, blue. Einstein's reaction to this was: this cannot be true. If you do a measurement on one side (the marble turns white), and something changes at the same time (marble turns blue); then that means that this happens faster than the speed of light and that is not possible. Nothing can travel faster than light, so this must be wrong.'

A. Riberi: 'So either things can travel faster than the speed of light or objects do not exist until we look at them?'

K. Susskind: 'Both seem to be true in the quantum world. As soon as observation takes place, the properties of an object are determined. The marble had no colour before we looked at it, but once it has been observed it will turn into one colour. And due to entanglement, one particle will immediately change as soon as the other changes and vice versa.'

A. Riberi: 'That is indeed very strange and quite difficult to comprehend.'

K. Susskind: 'And we are not there yet. We can go even further. Because not only do particles influence each other over great distances instantaneously, faster than the speed of light, but particles that were once together, for example within an atom, will always stay connected. This so-called non-locality phenomenon tells us that the dimensions of time and space do not exist in the world of the smallest.'

A. Riberi: 'Mr Susskind, it is getting a bit complicated now. What do you mean by non-locality and by the fact that the dimensions of time and space do not exist here?'

K. Susskind: 'Your Honour, as the example of the marbles shows, one of the most important principles of quantum mechanics is that two separate particles can affect each other instantaneously (the dimension of time does not exist anymore), regardless of where they are in relation to each other (the dimension of space no longer applies). We call this phenomenon non-locality.'

A. Riberi: 'Okay…'

K. Susskind: 'The deepest world of the smallest acts, as you say, very strange. And yet it happens.'

'At the end of the last century, this non-locality phenomenon was scientifically proven with photons (small particles of light) on the Canary Islands. On the island of La Palma, one photon was placed in a laboratory, the other photon was placed in a laboratory on Tenerife, 240 kilometres away. A third photon was then fused with the photon on La Palma so that its composition would change. And what happened? Exactly at the moment that the composition of this photon changed, the photon on Tenerife also changed, while there was no physical connection between the two.'

'In 2017, this test was repeated at an even greater distance, between the earth and a satellite that is located in space at 1,400 km. The result was the same, both photons connected to each other without any physical contact.'

'Einstein could hardly believe this and talked about 'ghostly interaction between two particles'. But maybe we are talking about 'teleportation at a distance' here, or about a multidimensional space where a particle that is in a certain dimension can in one way or another make direct contact with a particle in another dimension. Our research will give you more clarity as you will hear later on.'

A. Riberi: 'Okay, so if I may summarise: quantum particles, irrespective of location and observation by our consciousness, meet at a certain moment and will determine at that moment what happens in reality?'

K. Susskind: 'Yes indeed. I can explain this transfer of information between non-locality and consciousness with an example from the animal world.'

'Ant and bee colonies consist of creatures with different task assignments. At the same time, they have a group-consciousness that is coordinated by the queen. If we isolate the queen from the group alive (for example by putting her out of sight tens of kilometres away), the group continues its tasks. But if the queen is killed at that same distance (unseen by the other group members), chaos arises and all activities will be stopped immediately. The queen therefore coordinates all activities of the group at a distance (non-locally) by creating and maintaining a group-consciousness.'

'Another example can be found in transplants. As I just said, atomic particles that were once together, will always remain connected to one another. The donor organ contains the DNA of the donor. The DNA in the transplanted organ appears to serve as an interface with the donor's consciousness, so that the person receiving the organ can become aware of fragments of feelings or ideas that later seem to fit the personality of the deceased donor.'

'It is a fascinating theory that is barely comprehensible at times.'


A. Riberi: 'Thank you Mr Susskind. I suggest that we take a short break. As mentioned before, you are requested to stay inside the building. We will resume in half an hour.'

* * *

# CHAPTER 7

## In SITCO's laboratory - Colorado

## 6 weeks earlier...

I t is two weeks later, two weeks of preparation. We are all very impressed and excited. Solenn and I spend a lot of time together. I like her, I can identify with her ideas. She has a kind of pure way of being. She thinks in black and white, and is true to herself and to her thoughts.

She tells me about a touch of hands that she experienced a few months ago. Her mother had just died and she had thrown herself into her work. In the middle of the day, she had fallen asleep on the sofa and suddenly woke up when she felt two hands on top of her head. They put more and more pressure on her head, while she was already awake. There was no direct communication, there was no voice. Yet she felt she heard the words: 'it is good'. She looked around; there was no one in the house; where did this come from? It felt peaceful; was she in a dream or was this reality? She said it felt like some kind of Jesus figure was touching her. But this did not really fit into her philosophy of life. Through a friend she heard about the ALP and immediately signed up. She is curious to know whether we merge with some kind of divinity after death.

I tell her it could very well be the case that the whole universe and everything around us just consists of zeros and ones, and that, who knows, we are just being controlled by a joystick somewhere outside of space.

... It is time. Three persons in specially cooled coffins, attached to all kind of special medical equipment. Only white coats around us, tension in the air. First a partial cooling down of our bodies, followed by anaesthesia, then the incision of the aorta, then literally draining all the blood out of our veins, then repair of the aorta followed by the injection of some kind of special cold saline liquid in our veins, then remaining for 12 to 15 minutes in thermos bags at 2° C, followed by a connection to the heart-lung machine, receiving new blood, and the warming up of our bodies. It all sounds very straightforward but I am really starting to get freaked out now....

… The procedure has started; ice is placed around our bodies. I am overwhelmed by an unknown pain; it is so cold. It seems as if everything in my body is shrivelling up. I want to roll up, but I'm stuck and cannot move. I hear Isabela say 'bring back to 32° C'. The pain is getting worse, I am shivering all over my body. I feel small explosions, and muscles that are getting stiff from the tension... what have I got myself into ...

Then I feel the welcome injection in my arm, my eyelids start to feel heavy, and everything turns black ...

... Suddenly I am suspended below the ceiling. I see my body lying on a box with various people around it. There is a lot of blood. But I don't care, I don't feel any pain. I am as light as a feather and feel some kind of immense joy. I look at the other boxes, two more bodies, more blood. Suddenly I am standing on the other side of the wall in our sparse living area. The door to the laboratory is closed. What the …? Does that mean I went through the wall? I try it again and I am back in the laboratory; unbelievable.

I continue my journey and enter another room, some sort of large canteen. I look up and suddenly I am standing on the roof of the laboratory. It is so beautiful here. Mountain peaks and valleys all around me. Two birds are perched on the edge, singing. They stop when I get closer but they do not move. Do they notice my presence? Animals have a sixth sense, don't they? I try to call them but there is no sound. I look down and see that I no longer have a body as such. I find it strange, but I am not worried. Suddenly I am being drawn into a tunnel. It goes incredibly fast. It seems as though I am being pulled somewhere. I see all the colours of the rainbow around me. They are of an unknown intensity. The tunnel suddenly stops. In the distance I see a small dot of light, but I am pulled back the other way.

And then I am drawn back into my body again… The extreme cold is back…

\* \* \*

"Atoms never die.
It is like burning an encyclopedia,
information is not lost if one
keeps the smoke and the ashes.
It is just difficult to read."

Stephen Hawking

"The intuitive mind is a sacred gift
and the rational mind is a faithful servant.
We have created a society that honours the servant
and has forgotten the gift."

Albert Einstein

"If a tree falls in the woods and no ons is around to hear it,
does it make a sound?"

Anonymous

# CHAPTER 8

### 5 September 2036

New York - International Court of Ethics

Court hearing of the AfterLife Project

<u>Transcription - Afternoon of Day 1 - continued</u>

<u>Speakers</u>:     Antoni Riberi – Chairman of the Board

Kurt Susskind – Defendant

A. Riberi: 'Welcome back ladies and gentlemen. You have all seen the crowd that has gathered outside. As the police have their hands full, we have decided to shorten the session this afternoon, in the hope that the demonstrators will disperse more quickly afterwards.'

'Mr Susskind, if it is possible for you to finish your plea this afternoon, please do so. We could then continue on the next subject with your colleague tomorrow morning. The sooner we get all the information from you, the sooner we can come to a verdict on this issue, and the sooner the crowd outside will quieten down.'

K. Susskind: 'I will try to finish this afternoon, Your Honour.'

A. Riberi: 'Thank you. Please proceed.'

K. Susskind: 'As I told you before the break, there is chaos and uncertainty in the world of the smallest, and small particles influence each other at great distance. The laws of quantum mechanics are very different from the laws of the largest, where order and certainty are the rulers.'

'For decades, physicists have been searching for a method to unite the world of the largest with the world of the smallest. After all, there had to be a mathematical solution to chaos on the one hand and order on the other. But the force of gravity on one side, and the three quantum forces on the other side did not seem to match. And this was considered to be strange because they are both present in a black hole: gravity because the black hole is very heavy, and quantum physics because a black hole has a very small point in the centre where everything is sucked in, the singularity.'

'So, it was therefore necessary to find a theory, the so-called unification theory, which would apply to both the largest and the smallest and which could describe gravity at quantum level.'

'When string theory appeared in the 1970s, it was thought that this might be the unification theory.'

A. Riberi: 'What is meant by string theory?'

K. Susskind: 'To explain what a string is, we have to go back to atoms. If we break down an atom even further, we see that the core, the nucleus, consists of protons and neutrons, and these protons and neutrons consist of quarks. It becomes smaller and smaller. It was discovered around the 1970s that there are even smaller particles than quarks. These were called strings because they look like small vibrating particles; like mini-elastic bands.'

A. Riberi: 'So strings are the smallest particles that exist?'

K. Susskind: 'Not entirely, we recently discovered that there are even smaller particles. But according to the majority of physicists, the string is indeed the smallest possible particle.'

A. Riberi: 'Okay. Please continue.'

K. Susskind: 'Right, as I just said, a particle had to be found that could confirm gravity at the quantum level. Physicists called this particle a 'graviton'. In 1974, my namesake Leonard Susskind succeeded in mathematically calculating this graviton for the first time at the smallest (string) level.'

'This caused quite a stir because the missing piece of the puzzle had now been found mathematically. But although the graviton existed in theory, it took decades before its existence could actually be proven. And this was not easy because they had to look for a very specific string.'

A. Riberi: 'What do you mean?'

K. Susskind: 'According to the string theory, there are open and closed strings and multiple dimensions are possible. You could see a closed string as an elastic band that floats through space and is not attached to anything. An open string is a half elastic band that is attached to a piece of matter on one or both sides. The idea is that closed strings, as they float freely through space, could also move from one dimension to another. The graviton would also be such a closed string.'

Riberi: 'Okay…'

K. Susskind: 'Well, it was the CERN Institute in Geneva, Switzerland, that actually discovered the graviton in 2032.'
    'Are you familiar with this Institute?'

A. Riberi: 'This is where they do experiments with quantum particles, right?'

K. Susskind: 'Exactly. It is the European Research Centre for Particle Physics. There, in a 27-kilometre circular tunnel, atoms are collided with each other at almost the speed of light in order to see what happens to them.'

A. Riberi: 'And how did CERN discover the graviton?'

K. Susskind: 'They have not 'found' or 'discovered' the particle in the literal sense of the word of course, since it is far too small to see. They were able to demonstrate with measurements that one very small particle had disappeared in the collision between two particles. Since, according to the laws of nature, no energy can disappear, and since all other particles were open strings that were all attached to matter, this could only have been the graviton.'

A. Riberi: 'Okay…'

K. Susskind: 'Well, thanks to this discovery, the theories of gravity and quantum forces could now finally be brought together. And not only that, now that the graviton had disappeared this was also proof that multiple dimensions exist.'

A. Riberi: 'I do not quite follow you on that last part Mr Susskind.'

K. Susskind: 'Your Honour, I will try to explain it again.'
    'The particle accelerator in Switzerland allows particles to collide. In the event of a collision, very small nano (subatomic) particles are formed. It was hoped that, together with those particles, a little bit of gravity would arise: the graviton. We know, thanks to the string theory, that the graviton can move in other dimensions because it is a closed string, and it would therefore be scientifically possible to prove

that, if the graviton disappears, there would actually be extra dimensions. And this happened in 2032.'

'You may remember that the CERN Institute also received the Nobel prize for physics at the time?'

A. Riberi: 'Yes indeed, I remember something about that.'

'...Erm, you just mentioned that the graviton can move into other dimensions. What does that mean?'

K. Susskind: 'With other dimensions, you might think of parallel worlds besides ours, as my colleague Jack suggested. Other universes that may be very close to ours, but which we cannot perceive because our knowledge is limited to three dimensions plus the dimension of space-time. The hereafter could be in such a different dimension. We will tell you more about that later.'

A. Riberi: 'Okay. I have another question for you. You spoke earlier about the empty space in atoms and that all matter and even us human beings mainly consist of this empty space. Can you give us some further explanation; what exactly does this empty space mean, and what do we know about it?'

K. Susskind: 'This phenomenon of empty space in the universe and in all matter has indeed raised some big questions in recent decades. It is important to know that empty space does not necessarily mean that there is nothing; it is only that we cannot see what this space consists of. Just as the universe has different waves and rays, such as microwaves, X-rays, infrared rays and ultraviolet rays, which we cannot see or hear, the empty space is also filled with a certain type of energy that we cannot experience as such.'

'As you have already heard from my colleague Jack, the universe is largely made up of dark matter and dark energy. What has become clear in recent years is that there has been a misconception about dark space and empty space. It was assumed that it was the same. However, we have discovered that this dark space is not empty at all but is, on the contrary, full of energy. This space is also called the universal energy field. It is where a temperature of - 273.15° C is found, which is, as you may know, the coldest possible temperature, the absolute zero point, in the universe. It was thought that it could never get colder since atoms and molecules stop moving at this point and therefore no more energy could be released to produce matter. But our research has shown that there are ongoing vibrations behind this dark space (or dark energy), which means that there are actually vibrations below absolute zero.'

A. Riberi: 'So you say that all space around us that we experience as empty is actually not empty at all, but is full of vibrations and energy?'

K. Susskind: 'Yes, exactly. It may also be interesting to know that everything in the universe is actually based on these vibrations. All matter, plants, animals, objects, and even the human body consist of vibrations. All atoms and their even smaller particles are constantly moving. Inanimate objects such as stones vibrate more slowly, yet they do vibrate.'

'All our observations are focused on perceiving this rhythm, no matter which sense we are using. Perceiving vibrating sound waves (everything our ears hear) and vibrating light waves (everything our eyes see) are just two examples of this. Even the mechanism of the nerve cells that send information to our brain is characterised by the rhythmic pulsation of energy.'

'All these vibrations can be described as waveforms with vibrations per unit of time, also called frequency. Rhythms coincide when two waveforms of the same frequency run simultaneously with each other, meaning that the waves vibrate at the same time'.

A. Riberi: 'What do you mean?'

K. Susskind: 'I can give you a few examples that explain this phenomenon very well. First, we can look in a shop where they sell clocks from grandmother's days. Suppose not one of the clocks is wound up. If the pendulum is then set into motion and the clocks are wound up, the tick-tock movements will not run simultaneously. Over time, however, due to the transmission of vibrations, the clocks will all start to move back and forth in one movement. Their rhythms are therefore aligned at that time. This means that two vibrations, if they are close enough in terms of frequency, will eventually coincide.'

'There are other interesting examples, such as the experiment by a Harvard psychologist. A few years ago, she brought a group of people over seventy to a remote place, where an environment was created which was a replica of the year 1972. The furniture was matched to it, the wallpaper, the newspapers, the food, the music, the films, everything. A team of doctors found that the participants literally became younger after spending time there. Their finger joints became more agile, and their eyesight improved. Because the participants resonated with the information from 1972, not only their thoughts, but also their bodies began to adapt to the physical conditions of those days.'

'Another example comes from the plant world. Scientists experimented with the effect of noise and music on plants. Climbing plants were exposed to different musical styles during an experiment. And what happened? Climbers that heard works from Haydn, Beethoven, Schubert and Brahms every day grew towards the speakers or even around them. The plants that were exposed to Led Zeppelin and Jimi Hendrix grew away from the speakers, and even as far away as possible. So, you could say that, in the latter case, the plants did not really like that music! Or, in other words, that the frequencies of the vibrations were very far apart.'

'In the plant world, research has also shown that some plants can 'hear' vibrations. They 'hear' that caterpillars are coming to eat their leaves. They respond to this by secreting substances that could scare away the culprits. Some flowers even release their pollen only if bees make them vibrate at a specific frequency; so-called buzz pollination.'

A. Riberi: 'Interesting.'

K. Susskind: 'Yes, it is indeed an interesting matter. And the most interesting thing is that it is precisely this coincidence of specific vibrations that is needed to be able to look into the afterlife. It has become clear from our research that the frequency of the vibrations of the different dimensions (of the hereafter and earthly life, for example) are apparently not close enough to each other, or that we simply do not have the right senses to perceive these frequencies.'

A. Riberi: 'Right. Are you almost finished or are there any other issues you wish to discuss?'

K. Susskind: 'I think I have explained the most significant quantum principles to you. It is especially important that you remember the following basic rules:

'A wave (a series of possibilities) turns into a particle (into one possibility) when observation takes place. There is always uncertainty as to where the particles are exactly. They can disappear somewhere and reappear somewhere else, and be in different places at the same time (non-locality), where time and space play no role. In addition, particles can influence each other at great distances: if a particle changes, the associated antiparticle changes instantaneously, even if it is hundreds of kilometres away. And finally, particles that once belonged to each other will always remain connected (entanglement).'

A. Riberi: 'Thank you Mr Susskind. Tomorrow we will start at 9 a.m. with the next subject. Again, I ask for your discretion, and there should be no contact with the press. You will be guided through the back door to your accommodation by the agents present here. I wish you all a good night.'

\*\*\*

# CHAPTER 9

## New York Times - 6 September 2036

Yesterday was the first day of the hearing on the ethical issue of the 'AfterLife Project' at the United Nations headquarters in New York. We have learned from insiders that the actual research has not yet been discussed on this first day.

Thousands of demonstrators have gathered on the square in front of the United Nations. Some religious groups chant slogans against the research, human rights organisations demand a ban on the use of people as 'laboratory animals'. A small group of atheists and New Age followers argue for the continuation of the project. So far, the demonstrations have been fairly peaceful. The police made some arrests when Islamic and Jewish protesters started to fight but nothing else has been reported.

The question that occupies the mind is what the final decision of the Court of Ethics will be. The Court was already under attack in 2032 when it had to make a statement as to whether or not SpaceOne could continue sending people to planet Mars. After six failed space missions, killing all 28 astronauts, the Court finally decided in favour of SpaceOne, 'in the interest of technological progress'.

According to our correspondent in Colorado, there is a chaotic situation at the SITCO laboratory where the tests are being held. The laboratory is located at an altitude of 2,700 metres in the mountain village of Long Peaks, in the Rocky Mountains. Major traffic jams are reported on the road network around this small mountain village, which is normally only visited for its health and ski resorts.

According to social media, the laboratory is continuing with the tests. If this information is correct, the ALP organisation will be in a difficult position. Since September 1, they have been expressly forbidden to continue their research until the Court of Ethics has reached a verdict.

\* \* \*

# CHAPTER 10

*In SITCO's laboratory - Colorado*

*5 weeks earlier...*

I abela informs us about the results of the test. The most remarkable result was that of Indi, the woman in the wheelchair. Coming from England and at home in the world of meditation, she was more receptive to the experience than we were. She had gone deeper. She said that she had put herself in a state of meditation when the ice was spread over her body. As a result, she had felt virtually no pain. Her experience began with a feeling of an electrical stimulus just above her right ear. She felt that her essential self came out of her body through this point. She was suspended below the ceiling for a long time and saw a television just below her; the screen was facing towards her and a film was being shown. She thought it strange; nobody would be able to see the film unless they were watching from the ceiling. Isabela tells us that this was one of the controls to ensure that the near-death experience was real and not something that was being fabricated.

Indi's experience is very detailed. Whereas I went quickly through a tunnel and had actually only seen a variety of colours, she had seen much more. She had travelled past an infinite number of galaxies at an enormous speed. At the end of the tunnel, she had seen some kind of a horizon. There were other beings. Some of them she recognised, not by their appearance because there was no body as such, but by mutual feeling. She said that it felt very pleasant. She, who has been in pain for so many years due to her affliction with MS, was totally weightless and no longer felt any discomfort. She also felt the presence of Solenn but did not know where exactly she was. She said that she was attached to some kind of a stretchy elastic band. Then she was pulled back into the tunnel by this same band and returned to her body through the same point above her ear …

* * *

"Energy cannot be created or destroyed.
It can only be changed from one form to another.
Life is not the beginning
and death is not the end."

Albert Einstein


"What you have perishes,
What you are lives on,
beyond space and time"

Pim Van Lommel


"The distinction between the past,
present and future is only a
stubbornly persistent illusion"

Albert Einstein

# CHAPTER 11

## 6 September 2036

New York - International Court of Ethics

Court hearing of the AfterLife Project

Transcription - Morning of Day 2

Speakers:  Antoni Riberi – Chairman of the Board

Rosa Bernstein – Board member

Jack Brigance – Defendant

Léon Tautou – Defendant

A. Riberi: 'Good morning everybody. I hope that you all enjoyed a good night's rest and that you managed to get through the press and the crowd without too much trouble.'

'Mr Brigance, although you have already finished your plea, I would first like to start with you, since you are the director of the ALP. We have heard that your organisation is currently continuing with the tests, whilst this is strictly forbidden. What is your answer to that?'

J. Brigance: 'Your Honour, since we are currently here in New York, I unfortunately have no idea of what is happening in Colorado, but I find it hard to believe that what you are suggesting is true.'

A. Riberi: 'It appears that messages to that effect have been posted on social media by one of your employees. Of course, this could be fake news, but I would still offer you the urgent advice to sort this out as soon as possible.'

J. Brigance: 'I will Your Honour.'

A. Riberi: 'Thank you. Meanwhile, we will continue with the third plea. If I'm right, this one is about near-death experience and is given by you, Mr Tautou?'

L. Tautou: 'Thank you Sir, that is right.'
    'First, I would like to come back to what my colleague Kurt Susskind told you yesterday, namely that our body consists mainly of atoms and emptiness. Because it is actually a rather fascinating thought, isn't it, that if we take ourselves apart with a pair of tweezers, atom by atom, there would ultimately only remain a small pile of fine particles which, if they were reassembled would form a human body again, but only if they are reassembled in a certain way. This actually means that we are some kind of quantum pile ourselves;

a series of billions of ultra-small particles that are glued together. Unbelievable, don't you think?'

A. Riberi: 'Quite…'

L. Tautou: 'Well, you may know that our body consists of around 100,000 billion cells, and roughly one third of them die every two months. For example, if we take our skin cells, we lose about 50 million of them every day. They fall off our body all day long. Imagine how many skin cells swirl around us. It seems as though we are constantly walking in a cloud of our own death! Or imagine what it must look like microscopically on a bench in a public swimming pool. These benches are full of the dead skin cells of dozens of people … and we are just sitting on them without being aware of this! Hygiene… very important in a swimming pool!'

'Right, apart from that, it is fortunately the case that almost all cells renew themselves again and again during our lifetime. Within a few years, we are almost completely renewed, by 98%. Only certain cells in our eyes and brains remain unchanged.'

'But what happens at the end of our lives, when the atoms in our body fall apart and move on to be of use somewhere else? What happens to our essence, to our soul at that moment? When we die, will we just evaporate into thin air, or is there a continuity in another dimension, in a world other than this? What is death anyway and who is it exactly that dies? People who have had a near-death experience have a clearer picture of what happens after death.'

'I would like to take you along in order to look more closely at this interesting phenomenon. What is a near-death experience and what is happening in the brain at that moment? What exactly is consciousness, and where is the soul? These are some of the questions that will be answered in the coming days.'

A. Riberi: 'The floor is yours Mr Tautou.'

L. Tautou: 'Thank you Your Honour. Let me start with the most essential question: 'What exactly is a near-death experience?''

'Well, we speak of a near-death experience when someone enters a special state of consciousness, in which he is almost dead or in a situation of serious physical or emotional danger, beyond the earthly time-space boundaries. By time-space boundaries I mean that at that moment there is no longer a notion of time or space.'

'There are an estimated 25 million people in the world who have had a near-death experience. Many books about this phenomenon have been written by the well-known Raymond Moody, Kenneth Ring, Phyllis Atwater and Pim Van Lommel. Over the years, a long list of elements that these people encountered during such an experience has been drawn up.'

'Often they first step out of their bodies and then see their bodies from above. They can hear what bystanders or doctors are saying about them. They no longer experience pain in their bodies and they are aware that they are dead. They can be at another place at the same time and take a look back at their lives. Often, they go through a tunnel and are drawn at great speed to a small point of light. There they meet loved ones who have already died, or a being of light. There is a great sense of peace, love and acceptance. They have an awareness of omniscience. There is an experience of timelessness, everything happens at the same time. At the end of the experience, they arrive at a border that they cannot cross, after which they reluctantly return to their broken body.'

'Something else that these people always mention is the greatness of the experience. They often find it difficult to explain precisely what they have seen or heard because it cannot be compared to something that can be seen or heard here on earth.'

'The depth of the experience depends on the trauma suffered. About 20% of the people have a very deep experience. Most of the time, it involves a prolonged cardiac arrest or serious injury. In these cases, other experiences are added to the list. These people realise, for example, that there is a kind of string or elastic band that serves as a connection between their physical and astral bodies, and that the new body is reduced to a very small dot. They are aware that they consist of pure energy. They often see a kind of hourglass at the border, and get a preview of the rest of their live on earth.'

R. Bernstein: 'Mr Tautou, today I will be the one who will ask you most of the questions. Since somebody I know has had a near-death experience, I am probably more familiar with this phenomenon than my colleagues.'

'You talk about a physical and an astral body. I assume you mean that the perception of the body changes as soon as the person in question finds himself in this situation?'

L. Tautou: 'Yes indeed. People who have a near-death experience leave their physical body, or the body that consists of flesh and blood. They often float for a while above this physical body in a so-called astral body. Sometimes this is a transparent version of the physical body, but sometimes it is also reduced to a small point, and only contains their essence.'

R. Bernstein: 'Is it true that anybody can have a near-death experience or is this only for people who are very sensitive or religious, for example?'

L. Tautou: 'It can happen to anyone. As I just mentioned, most near-death experiences happen after severe physical trauma or cardiac arrest, but it can also happen to people who suffer from severe depression or who experience an emotional loss such as the death of a child, and even during dreams. Many studies on this phenomenon have shown that it can happen to men and women of all ages (including young children), who come from different cultures, and who have different professions and different religions.'

R. Bernstein: 'I see. There are, I believe, also people who have experienced a frightening or negative near-death experience and who have not experienced these beautiful elements, such as seeing loved ones and a being of light as you just suggested?'

L. Tautou: 'Yes indeed, although the percentage of negative experiences is very low, only 1 to 2 percent. These people talk of a dark space that they cannot leave and feel this as frightening. It appears that about three quarters of this group are people who have attempted suicide. During the near-death experience, they gain the insight that they are taking with them all the problems from which they wanted to flee. They experience that problems can better be solved during earthly life because the people with whom they have to solve them are here on earth.'

'There was one candidate in our research who had a frightening experience. During the test she had a positive and deep near-death experience and was so impressed that a few days later she tried to go back to that place by cutting her wrists. However, she ended up in a dark pit where she was being pulled down deeper and deeper. She saw a bright spot in the distance but felt that she was on another floor then during her first experience. She said that she was given the choice between returning to her body and solving her problems on earth and if her time had come, going directly to the bright light, or staying in this intermediate area and reaching the final light by crossing several floors, but that would be far more difficult. She saw other sad beings in this dark space; beings who had to stay there until their time had come to go to the other world. It was very uncomfortable and sinister. She chose to return to her body.'

'In addition, we had a candidate who described a negative experience she had as a teenager. She suffered from the eating disorder anorexia nervosa and since she did not eat, she often fainted. One morning she fainted but went much deeper. It seemed as though she was being pulled down into some kind of dark space. She saw her life passing by like an accelerated slide show. She felt heavy and anxious and called for help. She rose from the dark pit upon hearing her own voice.'

'Both women said that it was made very clear to them that committing suicide or challenging death is not allowed by the laws of the universe.'

R. Bernstein: 'If you say that suicide evokes a negative experience, what about your volunteers; are they not participating in an investigation that is not without danger, where they may face death? Is it not, in their case, a form of challenging death?

L. Tautou: 'No it is not. The volunteers are taking part in a test that is technologically so sophisticated that the risks are reduced to a minimum. Of course, there are always risks, but there are also risks in every hospital. A patient who does not wake up due to a medical error during an operation to remove his appendix is not seen as a suicidal person either, is he?'

R. Bernstein: 'And what about euthanasia? You could also see that as a sort of suicide?'

L. Tautou: 'Well, frankly, euthanasia indeed remains a big question mark.'

'As you know, there are different types of euthanasia, such as active euthanasia with a lethal injection; or assistance whereby a deadly drink or pills are provided. With passive euthanasia, the person chooses not to receive further treatment or resuscitation, stops taking antibiotics or refrains from eating and drinking. And there is also palliative care in a hospice.'

'As you know, active euthanasia is only permitted under strict conditions in a few countries, particularly in Europe. It could very well be that, with active euthanasia, the person who dies, will, just as those who attempt suicide, first end up in an intermediate station until their real day of death has arrived. Unfortunately, we do not know this. No near-death experience has been reported so far because euthanasia patients always die. What we do know is that people specifically ask for euthanasia because of the great fear they have of a painful dying process, and that in hospices in particular, the demand for euthanasia appears to be much lower when the patient is given morphine or any other kind of pain relief, so that the notion of pain is taken away.'

R. Bernstein: 'Understood. Let me ask you another question ...'

A. Riberi: Sorry to interrupt you, colleague, but I propose that we take a coffee break first. Let's resume in half an hour.'

\* \* \*

# CHAPTER 12

## *In SITCO's laboratory - Colorado*

## *4 weeks earlier*

Silence in the laboratory; a moment of reflection. Albert, one of the older men from the other group, has died during the test. What went wrong? We are told that he was terminally ill and only had a few months left to live. Everyone is surprised, was it the procedure itself? Was it his immune system that could not handle this treatment? Or did he perhaps want to determine the moment of death because of his incurably ill state, and was he able to choose not to return during his near-death experience? Questions without answers. The other older man, Angelo, who had undergone the test together with Albert, is very upset. He had noticed the presence of Albert after the tunnel at the light, and had felt that, at that moment, the string that kept them connected to the earth had broken on Albert's side. It was unclear to him whether this was due to circumstances or because Albert had chosen it himself. He did not feel that he had the choice of staying or going back. When he tried to get to Albert, he was pulled back into the tunnel…

Isabela tells us that the plans have now changed slightly. The idea is to restart the procedure in a week; this time only for Nathalie, with a maximum time of 20 minutes and a minimum temperature of 0.5° C. This means an even longer time in a near-death position and cooling down to an even lower temperature than us. This more severe test had already been tried with another group, but several participants had not returned alive. Those who had a near-death experience said that it was difficult for them to come back.

They would like to know why this is. It is up to Nathalie to find out what exactly happens after the journey through the tunnel. Why doesn't the elastic band reach further and why does it become weak or why does it let go? Why is it difficult to return, and does she have a choice or not?


…. Solenn and I spend the next week mostly together. She tells me about her near-death experience that was almost the same as mine except that she had also reached the horizon. She says that she has seen a large number of souls there, all were the same, there was no difference. Everyone was peaceful. It gave her a good feeling, it would probably mean that everyone is the same after death, that there is no difference between rich and poor, strong and weak, good and bad, no dualism.

She is a special woman, this Solenn. She cannot stand the abuse of power by people, or lies and hypocrisy. She has an increased intuitive sensitivity, a kind of sixth sense, knows immediately at the start of a conversation what the other person wants to say and whether or not they are speaking the truth. She says that she listens 'beyond' the spoken word, and understands why things happen in a certain way. She has a special connection with animals; according to her, the purest beings on earth. She is sometimes silent and absent, lost in thought. Talented, perhaps somewhat autistic, probably damaged by childhood traumas, but so pure and authentic that it is pleasant to be with her.

She tells me about her experiences in Antarctica, about the intelligence she has seen in animals. She finds it a real shame that so many people think that animals are not aware, that they do not have memories, or that they cannot anticipate future outcomes. If people would just give the animals a little more credit, they could learn a lot from them. Because could it not be true that animals communicate with each other at a completely different level? Are they not the ones with a very well-developed sixth sense and are they not the masters of intuition? Are they not the ones who know in advance that an earthquake is going to take place or that something bad is about to happen in the near future?

Solenn thinks that everything is connected through vibrations and energy. Animals probably feel these vibrations much better than we do. She is looking forward to the ultimate journey, then she might be able to get in touch with these vibrations...

* * *

"The think about brains is that
when you look into them, you discover
that there is nobody home"

Daniel Dennett

"I have noticed that even people who claim
that everything is predetermined and that
we can do nothing to change it,
still look before they cross the road"

Stephen Hawking

"The brain is only an instrument,
it is the mind that is this timeless expanding,
exploding intensity of creation"

Krishnamurti

# CHAPTER 13

## 6 September 2036

New York - International Court of Ethics
Court hearing of the AfterLife Project

Transcription - Morning of Day 2  - continued

Speakers:     Antoni Riberi – Chairman of the Board
              Rosa Bernstein – Board member
              Léon Tautou – Defendant

A. Riberi: 'Welcome back. Colleague Bernstein, please continue with your questioning.'

R. Bernstein: 'Thank you'.
    'Mr. Tautou, could it be that people fake a near-death experience?'

L. Tautou: 'That is an interesting question. Studies have shown that this is not the case. It is true that after taking certain drugs such as magic mushrooms, speed or LSD, or certain herbs such as Ayahuasca, people talk about a huge boost of energy or a feeling of bliss. They feel other vibrations around them where colours and matter merge. However, this experience in no way resembles a near-death experience, which goes much deeper and where people actually see that they are dead and where they are outside their body.'

'When a near-death experience occurs in an operating room for example, people can often recall exactly what was done during surgery, and which instruments (such as a drill or saw) were used on their body. Many details could be verified afterwards. Someone had, for example, jumped onto the roof of the hospital after his out-of-body experience, and had seen a red shoe lying there. This was indeed later verified to be true. It also happens that blind people can suddenly make visual observations and that colour-blind people can see all the colours of the rainbow. For more detailed information, I would like to refer again to Raymond Moody, who has carried out large-scale studies, and who has given many examples in his books of similar cases where people's experiences could all be verified afterwards.'

'In addition, in order to obtain an outcome that is 100% reliable, we take random samples, and have set up some scenarios in the laboratory that the candidates will only notice once they have left their bodies.'

R. Bernstein: 'Right. I understand what you mean when you say that there is a difference between taking drugs and having an esoteric experience after a major trauma. But perhaps there are also other causes for this stepping out of the body and the experiences mentioned by you? For example, could it not be a hallucination?'

L. Tautou: 'Some scientists who have not had intense discussions with people encountering a near-death experience, often remain convinced that there must be a classical scientific explanation for it. However, studies have clearly demonstrated that a near-death experience is not a hallucination nor a dream.'

'With a hallucination, the person in question sees a reproduction of himself. This image is projected onto reality, like a slide on a wall. The image that is seen is often misty and transparent. The person is a spectator and sees his projection moving in a lifelike way, as if he is watching a film of himself.'

'It is true that you could almost compare it to someone who has a near-death experience, who also sees his physical body as a spectator. There is, however one big difference: the person who has a near-death experience realises at that moment that he is dead. He sees a body below him which is no longer moving. Moreover, he can see what happens miles away from his abandoned body, and can check whether those events match with what really happened afterwards. Someone who hallucinates cannot do this.'

R. Bernstein: 'Could it be that a near-death experience is triggered by a deficiency of oxygen in the brain?'

L. Tautou: 'In the past decades, various leading cardiologists and neurologists have given possible scientific explanations for the near-death experience, but they all proved to be incorrect after careful examination. Oxygen deficiency in the brain was one such explanation, which has equally been proven to be incorrect.'

'When the heart stops, no more oxygen is pumped into the brain. The EEG then shows a flat line, and the person in question is clinically dead at that time. Without oxygen, the brain can normally only stay alive for a few minutes before it stops functioning. However, with many deep near-death experiences, people are sometimes resuscitated for up to 45 minutes. During this whole period of time, it seems as though the brain is in some kind of standby position. We will tell you how this is possible when we discuss our research.'

'In addition, we must not forget that there are also people who have a near-death experience without a physical trauma or cardiac arrest, and without a lack of oxygen in the brain, such as people suffering from a major depression.'

R. Bernstein: 'Yet it remains a fact that many medical specialists claim the near-death experience is only caused by brain trauma.'

L. Tautou: 'That is because these doctors think consciousness can only be found in our brain and that there is no such thing as an infinite or universal consciousness.'

R. Bernstein: 'What do you mean?'

L. Tautou: 'To understand this better, it might be useful to tell you a bit more about the structure of our brain first:'

'The brainstem is located at the lower back of the skull. The primitive survival functions are located here, such as balance, aggression, territorial urge and the hunt for food. The brain of a crocodile, for example, contains little more than a brainstem. That is why we call this the 'reptile brain'. In more evolved life forms such as mammals, we see that the brain has extended to the centre and front of the skull. They have, for example, a limbic system that is involved in emotions, motivation, joy and emotional memory. Animals that live in groups have a highly developed limbic system for understanding social rules and for organising hunting together. Finally, there is the prefrontal cortex, located at the front of the head, which is involved in cognitive and emotional functions such as making decisions, planning for the future and impulse control. Human beings are the only species on earth who have this prefrontal cortex.'

'Well, I think that one of the most important insights that the near-death experience has given us is that consciousness is not (only) the product of the brain, but that it is (also) located elsewhere in our body and everywhere around us. We know this not only because of studies into near-death experience, but also as a result of brain surgery in very young children who suffer from forms of epilepsy that are difficult to treat and where surgeons remove half of the brain.'

'As you know, the brain is divided into two separate halves: the right and left hemispheres. The left hemisphere controls logic, words and language as well as analytical skills. The right side controls creativity, artistic and musical skills as well as intuition. These children still have the same character after such brain surgery and can learn languages, play sports and be creative just like any other child. If consciousness were to be located in the brain only, how could you then explain that if half of the brain is taken away, the child can live on in a normal way without having changed at all? Or should we then say that consciousness was 'fortunately' seated in the remaining hemisphere? But either the left or right hemisphere is removed, so how can you explain that? The 17th century scholar Gottfried Leibniz suggested in his time that *"If you could enlarge the brain to the size of a workshop full of machines, and you would walk around in it, you would not encounter any consciousness"*.

'Another example can be found in people with a so-called split brain. In this case, the channel between the two hemispheres has been cut. Although these people often suffer from coordination problems after surgery, they are still fully aware of themselves and their environment in the same way as before, and they can lead a totally normal life.'

'I do need to make a small comment on these examples however. Both examples are about children and adults who have not suffered a major trauma. In the case of a brain injury due to a car accident, or in the case of a cerebral haemorrhage for example, there is a possibility that a person's personality changes because part of the brain no longer functions properly.'

'Apart from these two examples, we can also add that, if consciousness were indeed only produced by the brain, this would logically mean that consciousness should always disappear when the brain no longer shows any kind of activity.'

'However, near-death experience studies show that a different kind of consciousness is observed at the very moment (during clinical death) when the brain no longer shows any measurable activity and when functions such as body reflexes, brainstem reflexes and breathing have stopped. This consciousness can apparently be experienced independently of the brain and body at such a moment.'

R. Bernstein: 'Examples please, Mr Tautou.'

L. Tautou: 'Well, if we look at geniuses such as Mozart, Beethoven or Einstein, for example, then it really cannot be anything other than they were somehow connected to this non-local infinite consciousness. If we take someone like Mozart, who was able to play very difficult pieces and compose complex pieces of music at the age of 5; he must have had access to the entire music spectrum of universal consciousness, as how could a child of that age otherwise have such incredible skill? Einstein said that he simply 'received' the general theory of relativity. And Mozart's famous words in a letter to his father were: 'All music is already there, it just needs to be written down'.

'Another example is autistic people. Those with an autistic savant syndrome often have special knowledge in a certain area. For example, they have mathematical ability that does not seem rational, they can perform very complicated calculations in no time, or learn entire telephone directories by heart within a couple of hours.'

'We are all connected to the universal consciousness, but certain people have more extensive access to certain parts of it than others. The above-mentioned geniuses were able to lead an ordinary life because the rest of their individual consciousness was intact, but with autistic people it is a little different. For some of them, the part that has the upper hand (for example, the part governing logic and mathematics) takes over from the rest of the individual consciousness, as a result of which they cannot function as well in other areas and are often in need of care.'

R. Bernstein: 'Mr Tautou, it is getting a bit complicated now, could you explain more about this universal consciousness that is present everywhere?'

A. Riberi: 'Sorry to interrupt you again, respected colleague, but I suggest that we first take a lunch break before going any further. We will resume at 2 p.m.'

\* \* \*

# CHAPTER 14

## *In SITCO's laboratory - Colorado*

## *3 weeks earlier...*

Everything is ready. Nathalie is laying in an iced coffin. Medical staff in white coats are spreading more ice on top of her. Now that Indi, Solenn and I have recovered sufficiently, we are allowed to be present during the procedure. It is strange to experience this from the other side now.

After a couple of minutes, Nathalie starts to shiver and her teeth begin to chatter. A special bit is put in her mouth so that she cannot hurt herself.

As soon as the temperature of 32° C is reached, they give her an anaesthetic and open up her carotid artery. I shrink back; blood is spraying in all directions. A couple of litres are collected in large bins that had been placed underneath her neck.

They work quickly. A special saline solution is administered in Nathalie's veins after which she is placed in ice cold thermos bags until she has cooled down to 0.5° C.

Then we have to wait. 20 long minutes…

…The clock ticks slowly. 9 minutes, then 10. It is as though we are looking at a corpse. Grey skin, sunken cheeks, very thin arms and legs, and a sort of macabre smell of blood pervades the air.

15 minutes pass by, 16. Nathalie suddenly starts to shake uncontrollably. Everybody rushes over to her. The procedure is now being applied inversely. Blood is added in her veins, and she is warmed up and connected to the heart-lung machine.

No reaction.

Isabela gives her an electric shock.

Still a flat EEG.

Extra saline solution is administered followed by another electric shock.

No response.

'Come on girl', Isabela shouts and gives her a third shock. The EEG shows a small uneven line, Nathalie's heart starts to beat irregularly.

Everyone holds their breath. Nathalie's blood pressure is slowly going up again, but it is not there yet. Her body is still way too cold and has trouble returning to its normal temperature. A special thermal blanket is wrapped around her and even more saline fluid follows.

After 30 minutes, Nathalie's body is reasonably up to temperature again, but she does not give any response to impulses. Is she in a coma? …

* * *

"What if you slept?
And what if in your sleep you dreamed?
And what if in your dream you went to heaven
and there plucked a strange and beautiful flower?
And what if when you woke up
you had that flower in your hand?
Ah, what then?"

Samuel T. Coleridge

"The whole world yearns after freedom,
yet each creature is in love with his chains;
This is the first paradox and inextricable
knot of our nature"

Sri Aurobindo

"What if life is a dream,
And as you can awaken from a dream,
You can also awaken from life?"

Anonymous

# CHAPTER 15

## 6 September 2036

New York - International Court of Ethics
Court hearing of the AfterLife Project

Transcription - Afternoon of Day 2

Speakers:    Antoni Riberi – Chairman of the Board
             Rosa Bernstein – Board member
             Léon Tautou – Defendant
             Jack Brigance - Defendant

A. Riberi: 'Welcome back everybody. Mr Brigance is also in our midst once again, I see. Let me start with you. What is the latest news?'

J. Brigance: 'Your Honour, Members of the Board, apologies for my absence. It appears that a number of demonstrators have tried to enter our laboratory. This means that all safety systems have been activated and the communication network has shut down. Even the mobile network is not functioning at this moment. This is why, unfortunately, I have not yet been able to contact my colleagues.'

A. Riberi: 'I indeed learned during our lunch break that there are some problems with your laboratory. It is strange though that you cannot contact one of your colleagues by mobile phone. The mobile network is separate from the computer network, I should think. Surely it must be possible to reach somebody one way or another?'

J. Brigance: 'Well…'

A. Riberi: 'So you still don't know if the tests are going on?'

J. Brigance: 'Even though no communication is possible at this very moment, I can assure you that no tests are currently being done.'

A. Riberi: 'As you understand, we would like to receive an answer directly from the laboratory. I therefore request that you continue your efforts to get in touch with one of your employees this afternoon.'

J. Brigance: 'Very well.'

A. Riberi: 'Mr Tautou, my colleague Mrs Bernstein asked you before the lunch break what you mean by a non-local universal consciousness that is present everywhere? Please proceed.'

L. Tautou: 'Thank you, Your Honour.'

'Consciousness actually means realising, or being aware of oneself and the environment. Consciousness is formed by a combination of impressions from the outside world on the one hand and emotions, thoughts and feelings from our inner world on the other. At the moment something is being experienced, the brain combines this with experiences from the past, with the associated feelings, thoughts and emotions, and what is happening in the outside world at that very moment, such as for example a person saying something, an object that is seen or a sound that is heard, et cetera.'

'As my colleague Kurt said earlier, we think that what we experience is reality but this is actually not true. What we experience is actually an illusion created by our brain. Let me explain. We are all shaped by the influences of our parents, environment, school, religion et cetera. Everyone experiences his own youth in a certain environment. The moment someone experiences something, the brain automatically adds experiences from the past and then compares these with what is going on at that moment. Since the experiences of the past are different for everyone, the truth of what is actually being experienced can therefore only be considered subjectively.'

'Our research has clearly shown that there is an infinite or universal consciousness beyond everyone's individual consciousness. Other names are cosmic consciousness or unity consciousness. It is a consciousness to which we, as earthly beings, are attached as little puppets and to which we only have partial access.'

R. Bernstein: 'Can you be a bit more specific and give us some examples?'

L. Tautou: 'The best way to explain this further, would be to compare the universal consciousness with modern communication.'

'As you know, there is a continuous exchange of information via, for example, smartphones, television and the Internet, where time and distance do not play a role. This is due to electromagnetic information waves that travel at the speed of light. We only need to press a button and the information is available. These waves are all around us, but we are only aware of them when we switch on the mobile phone, television or computer. What we receive is not in the device itself. The voice that we hear on our mobile phone is not in the telephone. The TV broadcast is not in the TV set. It is only when you switch on the TV that you will see the programme, when you switch it off you no longer see it, but the broadcast still continues.'

'Hundreds, maybe thousands of programmes are being broadcasted worldwide at the same time, but we can only see one programme at a specific time and place, that is how limited we are with our senses.'

'Another example is the Internet. A computer makes it possible to receive millions of different websites. The computer itself does not produce these websites; it is only a channel for the information. As soon as you switch off the computer, you no longer have access to the websites. However, the websites still exist.'

'You can see the universal or infinite consciousness as these TV programmes or these websites, and the brain as the TV or the computer. In the universal consciousness, all knowledge is present; it is not visible, but as soon as you press a certain button (of a certain memory for example) that specific information is immediately there. Our brains act as a channel. They do not have a producing but a facilitating role for consciousness.'

'One of our candidates puts it as follows. She compared the universal consciousness with a huge department store where all possible things and facts are displayed on thousands of shelves. During our lifetime, this department store is shrouded in the dark and we can only see a very limited part around us with a flashlight. During a near-death experience (and after death), the entire department store is completely illuminated all at once; everything is visible at once and people know and understand everything at once.'

'As early as the 14th century, the Jewish scholar and philosopher Narboni mentioned that a fusion would take place with the 'universal intellect'. He said that, through the pursuit of knowledge, the soul will be united in this earthly life with the 'universal intellect', and that, at the moment of death, it will lose all its individuality and identity to completely merge with that higher intelligence.'

R. Bernstein: 'Mr Tautou, how are you so sure that this infinite consciousness actually exists?'

L. Tautou: 'It has to be, it cannot be otherwise than that it does exist. When you consider that our brain is made up of pure matter, of cells that are constantly being renewed; if you also realise that the brain only has a limited information capacity, then storage must take place elsewhere.'

'Our brain consists of 100 billion neurons. Each neuron has hundreds to thousands of synapses that ensure the connection with other neurons. The brain has no knowledge until connections are made between neurons.'

'You can see all these connections as a huge network of superimposed roads where all roads are connected to each other with roundabouts. But even though the storage capacity of this network is large, it is completely inadequate for storing all our memories with the associated thoughts and emotions. It is simply anatomically and functionally impossible, as has been demonstrated by various neurologists and computer experts.'

'You can also compare it with a computer. This also has a maximum memory capacity. When the maximum amount of memory is used, new information can no longer be added and the computer crashes.'


'Apart from this technical explanation, I can also give you a completely different example of the non-local consciousness. It concerns people who have suffered a brain haemorrhage.'

'As you know, a brain haemorrhage is caused by a vein bursting in the brain. Blood then flows freely into the brain matter. People who experience this can suddenly no longer produce any normal sentences or have a terrible headache and start to vomit. The magnitude of the damage will only become clear later on an MRI scan.'

'A prominent American neurologist, after experiencing a haemorrhage in her left hemisphere, said that when this part of her brain (with logic and rational thinking) failed, she ended up in a completely different world. She said there was no clarity anymore as to where her own body stopped and where the bricks of the wall in her room began, everything had become one big swarm of fused atoms. The sense of time and space had disappeared, she found herself in one big 'now'. She experienced herself as liquid, as huge, as pure consciousness, fused with everything around her.'

'From several similar stories, it has become clear that if the left hemisphere no longer functions, there are no more obstacles to directly getting in touch with the universal consciousness. Apparently, our logical left brain, that thinks in boxes, prevents us from establishing this connection.'

R. Bernstein: 'Okay, so you say that this external consciousness must exist and that we will experience it in its entirety as soon as we die, if I understand correctly?

L. Tautou: 'Yes indeed.

R. Bernstein: Okay, but what about our sleep? Isn't it also suggested that sleep can be seen as 'the little death', that there is a period during our sleep where consciousness cannot be detected? Could it be that, at that moment we are connected to this external consciousness?'

L. Tautou: 'That is a very good question. You know that our sleep consists of different phases?'

R. Bernstein: 'Yes but I do not know the exact details.'

L. Tautou: 'Well, our sleep consists of five phases. It starts with the transitions phase (floating in and out of consciousness), followed by light sleep, the transition from light to deep sleep, deep sleep and REM sleep. Over the course of the night, the body will go through this five-stage cycle four to six times, spending an average of 90 minutes in each stage, during which the REM sleep becomes increasingly shorter after each cycle. During deep sleep, our breathing and heartbeat are at their lowest. On an EEG, the brain only shows very large and slow wave movements at this moment.'

'This deep sleep is the most interesting stage for us. In the 1920s, the brain was thought to erase unnecessary memories at night. A study showed that when mice were asleep, the number of connections between their brain cells decreased by around 18 percent. During the day, the number of these synapses increased again because the animals gained new experiences and formed memories.'

'Further research has shown that, in people, the number of connections between brain cells during sleep also decreases. However, during this 'trimming process', part of the memories gained are not erased, as was previously suggested, but they are moved to the consciousness that lies outside our brain in large energy fields.'

'As soon as a person is awake and something happens, all relevant experiences of the past arrive in the brain in just a few hundredths of a second and the synapses at that moment provide so many connections between the neurons that, bit by bit, all pieces of the puzzle fall into place. In other words, through one of our senses (such as seeing, hearing or feeling) the right thought is picked from the energetic field around us. This thought is then connected to other thoughts in the brain through the synapses and neurons, until finally the picture is complete and correct.'

'It is the information for the long-term memory that is stored outside our brain in particular.'

'You could compare this process with storing computer documents in the 'cloud'. You create a document and save it in the 'cloud'. As soon as you want to see the document again, you only have to push a button. The 'cloud' is at a non-local level; you can access it from anywhere at any time as long as you have a computer. This is also the case with our memories. You only have to think about a detail for a moment, it doesn't matter where you are, or what time it is, and all the feelings, ideas and emotions of that experience will appear immediately 'from the cloud'.'

R. Bernstein: 'So in other words, during our sleep our brain is cleaning up?'

L. Tautou: 'Yes, that is right. During deep sleep, the things that happened during the day and the new things learned are stored outside our brain in energetic fields. If this did not happen, our brain would very quickly not be able to absorb any new information and, just like a computer, would start to crash due to lack of capacity, as previously mentioned.'

'People who do not sleep well will certainly recognise this problem. With superficial or light sleep, where one wakes up over and over again, only four of the five sleeping phases will occur, the real deep sleep is missing. Or when one lies awake for hours before falling asleep, the deep sleep will come along, but there are not enough cycles to go through the trimming process as a whole. The result is that these people are very tired and unable to concentrate during the day because the trimming process has not been adequate and the 'disk' in their head is already almost full in the morning.'

R. Bernstein: 'Okay, so if I follow you correctly, a large part of the information gathered by our daily experiences is stored outside our individual consciousness?'

L. Tautou: 'Yes indeed.'

R. Bernstein: 'Okay I see.'

'In addition to our individual consciousness, there is also a subconsciousness that is sometimes compared to an iceberg, where the top of the iceberg that rises above the water is seen as the conscious and the part under water the subconscious. Is that correct?'

L. Tautou: 'Yes, that is true. And it must be said that the part of the iceberg under water is more than 90 percent and the part above water is less than 10 percent. The subconscious part is much larger than the conscious part. In other words, our conscious part knows very little about reality.'

'The subconscious part captures 22 million bits of information per second, whereas our conscious only perceives 50 to 100 bits per second. And ... these paltry 50 to 100 bits are also coloured by our senses, because, as I said earlier, the senses dig for similar past experiences and thus put their stamp on what the reality of today should look like approximately. We can therefore conclude that the truth of our observations is really very far away.'

R. Bernstein: 'In addition to the conscious and subconscious, there is also such a thing as waking consciousness, right?

A. Riberi: 'Colleague Bernstein, I am going to interrupt again. Let's take a short break and continue the questioning in half an hour.'

\* \* \*

# CHAPTER 16

*In SITCO's laboratory - Colorado*

*10 days earlier...*

Five scientists are looking with serious faces at a large screen on one of the walls of the meeting room. Jack Brigance stands up and gestures towards the screen:

'Good morning, dear colleagues. This is our last meeting before the trial in New York begins. As you can see on the screen, there is still a lot of speculation going on on social media about the possible outcome, and especially that it will probably not be to our advantage. The interference and negativity we have received from certain religious communities over the past few months seems to have paid off. Apparently, spiritual leaders in Rome and the Middle East still hold a very dominant position in this world. We just have to wait and see how the members of the Court are going to approach us and what kind of questions they will come up with.'

'I think we all agree on one thing though: our journey continues no matter what. We are too close now to withdraw. Now that the renewed nanochip is ready, the vitrification method will certainly succeed. Kurt, could you give us the latest update?'

Kurt stands up and sweeps with his right hand from left to right on an invisible screen in front of him so that a new picture appears on the wall:

'The TP-5 is a very powerful chip with ultra-thin nanowires. It acts as a superconductor between the brain of our candidates and our quantum computer G. Specially placed photons in the chip and in G will influence each other from a distance, making it possible to transfer information between the brain of the candidates on the one hand and the computer on the other, no matter what the distance and time frame may be.'

'The chip is placed in the brain of the candidates and then linked to G's program. If all goes well, the candidate in question will now be able to release the elastic cord to which they are attached when they reach the border during a near-death experience, then cross the border and still remain connected to earthly life… Look, here we have an image of the TP-5.'

Kurt points his finger at an enlarged image of a peanut on the screen.

Isabela is only half-listening, as she is still with Nathalie in her thoughts. Fortunately, her situation has improved. Yesterday, she opened her eyes again for the first time. She had a smile on her face and said that it was not her time yet, and that she still had to complete certain tasks on earth. She was very tired. When asked if something had happened to the elastic cord, she said that it had become thinner the longer she stayed there. At one point, it was so stretched that it almost broke. A voice then told her to go back, and pushed her into the tunnel. She had pulled on the cord but it was so weak that she had tumbled down. It was as if she had lost her grip. The creature of light that had previously pushed her now held her so that she would not fall down further. The touch had been breathtaking. It had felt as if the creature and she had been intertwined, had been one. Then she had returned to her body but could not get in touch with the outside world.

Well, only up till now, she was glad to be back. It had been an amazing journey, and she now knew what she had to do in the coming years. 'You are doing a good job, Isabela', she had said, 'everyone should know what it looks like over there ...'

Kurt walks back to his chair with a gesture towards the screen: '... And G will then further analyse the information sent by the chip with this specific program; we do not know exactly how it will do this, probably by means of symbols as I just explained ... '

Isabela looks at the screen and sees an ever-growing snowflake, each new piece showing the same symmetrical pattern as the earlier pieces in the middle. At the bottom of the screen she sees the word 'Fractal'.

Jack Brigance stands up: 'Let's wrap things up for now. As agreed, Robert will place the chip in the brain of the candidates and Kurt will link it to the qubits of G. Then the four of us will leave for New York. Isabela stays here in the laboratory.'

He goes to Isabela and gives her a small ring.

'Keep this with you at all times. Kurt and I both have one too. It is a very advanced device with which we can stay in contact in the coming period should the other communication channels be blocked or intercepted for some reason. You just have to press the blue sapphire to connect. If we contact you, you will feel a slight vibration on your finger. The connection is coded and cannot be traced …

\* \* \*

"A rose is but a rose,
It blooms because it blooms
It thinks not for itself, nor
asks if it is seen"

Angelus Silesius

"I see now that I am asleep
and that I dream that I am awake"

Pedro Calderòn de la Barca

"What is a good man but a bad man's teacher?
What is a bad man but a good man's job?"

Lao Tse

# CHAPTER 17

## 6 September 2036

New York - International Court of Ethics

Court hearing of the AfterLife Project

Transcription - Afternoon of Day 2 - Continued

Speakers:    Antoni Riberi – Chairman of the Board

Rosa Bernstein – Board member

Léon Tautou – Defendant

A. Riberi: 'Welcome back.'

'Mr Tautou, my colleague asked you before the break if, apart from our conscious and subconscious, there is such a thing as a waking consciousness. Please proceed.'

L. Tautou: 'Thank you Your Honour. Yes, the waking consciousness indeed exists. According to the famous psychologist Carl Jung, our 'I' is our waking consciousness, and our 'self' is a wider aspect around the 'I' that includes both the conscious and the subconscious part of the personality. Certain aspects of the subconscious can only be experienced through dreams, meditation or hypnosis. According to Jung, the collective subconscious (or, in other words, the infinite consciousness) will never even be accessible from our waking consciousness. But that view has now been revised.'

R. Bernstein: 'You said earlier that consciousness actually means 'being aware'. But if I understand your other line of reasoning, there are actually two meanings associated with the same word: consciousness that can be seen as a noun, and 'being aware' that can be seen as a verb. Do you think both are the same or is there a difference?'

L. Tautou: 'The verb 'to be aware' is actually a synonym for the art of being fully awake. For example, if I sit with two other people on a couch watching television, then one person will see a landscape, the other a beautiful blue sky, and I will see a butterfly flying at the bottom of the screen, for example. We all look at the same images but all see something different, we are all aware of something else.'

'If we were totally aware at that moment, we would not only notice a blue sky, a screen, a landscape and a flying butterfly at the same time, but we would also see the cat walking through the door, hear a car start outside, hear the dishwasher turn off, feel the warm rays of the sun shining through the window on our face, and taste the apple pie we have just eaten in our mouth ... That is 'being totally aware'.'

'Consciousness as a noun is, in our opinion, a much larger thing; a universal and infinite event that is all around us.'

R. Bernstein: 'Our consciousness also includes our thoughts, right? What are thoughts in your opinion and are they located somewhere in our brain or also somewhere 'non-local'?'

L. Tautou: 'Thoughts can be compared to clouds on the horizon. They appear and disappear spontaneously. Thoughts are often about the past or the future and appear when something stirs them up. They arise in the non-local space, and our brains act as a conduit or channel.'

R. Bernstein: 'Okay that is clear. Another question. You mentioned earlier that past, present and future happen simultaneously during a near-death experience. Does that mean that time stops at that moment?'

L. Tautou: 'Time is something that we only experience as such here on earth. People who are having a near-death experience, experience a great deal, even with a cardiac arrest lasting a few minutes. They relive all the details of their past life with all the associated emotions. And not only that, they also feel the emotions of the people with whom they shared the experiences, and see and feel what the consequences of their actions were.'

'For earthly time concepts, it would be impossible to experience so much in a time span of just a few minutes.'

'So, we see here that everything that is experienced at that moment is independent of our earthly time frame. Everything seems to exist and be experienced at the same time as soon as attention is drawn to it.'

R. Bernstein: 'So, just as your colleague Susskind suggested that time and place do not exist at quantum level, you say that people experience this same non-existence of time during a near-death experience?'

L. Tautou: 'Yes exactly. It appears that everything and everyone is timelessly connected at that moment, and one can be everywhere at the same time. You can also read about this phenomenon in the books of Raymond Moody. People who are suddenly standing in their parents' living room during a near-death experience by just thinking about them, while these parents often live hundreds of miles (and sometimes even half a continent) away.'

R. Bernstein: 'You just mentioned that, during their life overview, these people are connected to other people's consciousness. What do you mean by that?'

L. Tautou: 'During a near-death experience, one feels the emotions of all persons involved in their actions. For example, if they bullied someone in their youth, they will experience it again and feel what it did to the other person, and what the consequences were for that person and for all those around him.'

'Studies also show that people who have committed a lot of crimes or a murder for example, get a more difficult and larger life overview. The consequences of their actions have had such a big impact, and there are so many people involved who have been suffering, that these people have to deal with a lot of emotions of sadness, misunderstanding, anger et cetera.'

'All in all, it shows that we are one hundred percent responsible for our actions.'

'One of our candidates said that he experienced it as being his own judge and executioner at the same time. He experienced the pain, the anger, the helplessness and sorrow of all the people who had felt these emotions through his actions, and saw what he had done wrong and what he could and should have done differently.'

'In addition, it is interesting to know that there is no judgement by a divine being, which is often preached by religions. Raymond Moody put it as follows in one of his books: *It is interesting to know that in every case I studied, it was not the essence of light that judged, but it was the people themselves who acted as judges and gave themselves a judgment for actions taken.*'

'As you remember, my colleague Jack Brigance spoke about our goal at the beginning. Well, if we can reach the average citizen in the world through our presence here, and encourage them to be open to near-death experiences and to this kind of important information, then one might be more inclined to act more cautiously from now on, knowing that every action will have its consequence. One might think twice before proceeding with actions that will have far-reaching consequences, such as abuse or violence.'

R. Bernstein: 'A nice thought, Mr Tautou, but perhaps a bit idealistic, don't you think?'

L. Tautou: 'Everything is possible.'

R. Bernstein: 'I have a very different question for you about consciousness. And even though we deviate slightly from the theme here, I would still like to ask it and hear your opinion.'

'As you know, robotisation has shown exponential growth in recent years, and machines are now able to perform many jobs in banks and hospitals. There has been speculation for decades regarding whether or not a robot can have its own consciousness. I am curious as to what you have to say about this. Suppose that robots can create their own consciousness in the near future, will they then have access to this infinite consciousness in one way or another?'

L. Tautou: 'An interesting question, Mrs Bernstein. Many computer experts believe that consciousness will develop of its own accord as technology progresses. Like many other scientists, they hold that consciousness is a product of the brain that can be simulated by a robot. However, as you now know, consciousness is something far wider than just receiving and processing information. Creativity, for example, is something that cannot be learned with logic or through formulas, and in the same way, experiencing a feeling of freedom or a feeling of joy cannot be learned.'

'Having said that, let's not forget that today's quantum computers have so much knowledge that you might be tempted to think they are all-knowing. However, there is one big difference between them and us: even the most advanced quantum computers have no knowledge of death, of the hereafter or of multiple dimensions in the universe. Nor do I think these computers or robots will ever know or experience this.'

'But… you never know where the technology will take us in the future. If robots are indeed sent out into space at some point in time because they can travel as little nanochips at the speed of light and thus traverse the entire universe in less than 50 years, then they may receive all kinds of new information from distant galaxies and from black holes, and perhaps develop a new form of consciousness.'

'A robot will, however, never be able to create the kind of consciousness that we experience.'

R. Bernstein: 'To continue on this side track, the human being of today has conquered many diseases. Thanks to immune therapy in recent years, diseases such as cancer have now become chronic disorders.'

'We are monitored daily by our smartphone, and we immediately know if something is wrong with our body and, if so, what we should do about it. In the past decade, the average age of people has risen to more than 100 years, and there are now people still alive who are older than 135 years.'

'Did anything come up about this phenomenon in the near-death experiences? Is it true that human beings will get older and older and, at some point, will no longer have to die because we can renew the cells in our body thanks to advanced technology?'

L. Tautou: 'Various near-death experiences have shown that the human beings of today are psychologically unable to live for such a long time. Cells in our body can indeed be replaced by new ones, but our brain stays behind.'

'The intelligence of the average person has increased more and more as we grow older and older. As a result, as you know, a new illness has arisen in the past decade, the successor of the well-known burnout, EBS, the so-called 'Exploded Brain Syndrome', in which the patient 'pops out of his skull'. A very painful disease.'

'Too much information, excessively high intelligence, and evolution of the brain that progresses too slowly, considering the rapid exponential growth in technology and information. People turn into frightened zombies.'

'Certain parts of the brain such as the amygdala and the hippocampus, which, among other things, regulate emotions and short-term information storage, weaken in such a way that the abundance of information causes extreme stress and makes people confused and disoriented. They walk down the street no longer knowing what they are doing or where they are going, with all the consequences this brings. A nasty disease, which, unfortunately, cannot be cured yet with medication and can currently only be suppressed by using electro-shocks.'

R. Bernstein: 'Yes, EBS is indeed a nasty neurological disorder. So, you are saying that we are becoming smarter but cannot handle the large amount of information we receive every day?'

L. Tautou: 'Yes indeed, we cannot properly streamline the amount of information. We could compare this to the binary computer and the quantum computer, where the binary computer represents our life here on earth and the quantum computer represents the universal consciousness. The binary computer code can only do its calculations with a 1 or a 0, but never with a 1 and a 0 at the same time. The same applies to us. Our earthly life film runs on a timeline from left to right, from past through present to future. One event happens after the other. It is just like a slide show, everything follows on from something else, slide after slide. As human beings, we cannot help but live in this binary way: things happen one after the other, and the knowledge gained must be filtered at night to make room for new knowledge the next day; otherwise our brain gets stuck and we become ill.'

'In the quantum world it is the other way around. Everything can happen at once. Quantum computer qubits can be 0 and 1 at the same time. The same applies to the universal consciousness; there is no past, present or future, and everything happens at once.'

R. Bernstein: 'If you compare the universal consciousness to a quantum computer, are you then suggesting that there may be a mathematical calculation behind the entire creation?'

L. Tautou: 'Who knows! Perhaps as human beings we are simply transitional figures that will evolve to a world of machines. It may very well be that we are no more than 'intelligent avatars' in some cosmic computer simulation of a super intelligent species, and that we end up as cyborgs, a fusion of man and machine.'

R. Bernstein: 'But is this not at odds with what you just said about the near-death experience?'

L. Tautou: 'To be honest, the one does not exclude the other. Everything could very well be based on little energy packages that are broadcast by some sort of supernatural computer intelligence.'

'But, of course, we could also adopt a completely different approach. Let us assume, for example, that Darwin is correct with his theory of evolution: that it is not the strongest and smartest who have the best chance of survival, but the most adaptive. We have seen it happen throughout history in the animal world; those who won the struggle for survival are those who could best adapt to a new situation.'

'Now, it may very well be that man returns to earth time and time again, during which the earthly consciousness is becoming smarter and smarter, and man adapts himself to this newly acquired intelligence, until a point is reached where there are only two possibilities: either man becomes a super intelligence and melts and merges with artificial intelligence or man exterminates himself and the universal game starts all over again, but with other forms of life.'

'Anyway, the only thing we have been able to determine through our research is that there is an infinite consciousness with which we will all be united after death, whether this energy consists of zeros and ones or not.'

A. Riberi: 'Thank you Mr Tautou. I propose that we leave it here for now and continue tomorrow. Just like yesterday, you will be escorted to your accommodation by the police. I wish you all a good night's rest and I look forward to seeing you here again tomorrow morning at 9 a.m. And we hope to receive a clear answer from you then, Mr Brigance.'

\* \* \*

# CHAPTER 18

## New York Times - 7 September 2036

Yesterday, the second day of the trial of the 'AfterLife Project' took place at the United Nations headquarters in New York. According to our source, the research itself has still not been discussed.

On the square in front of the United Nations headquarters, the situation is becoming grimmer by the minute. More and more activists are gathering, especially now that the rumour is spreading on social media that not only the tests are going ahead as normal in Colorado, but that it concerns the controversial vitrification method. We have asked SITCO for clarification, but they have not yet responded.

Supporters of Cryo-conservation have now joined the atheists and New Age supporters. They are in favour of the project. The Cryos, as they call themselves, consist mainly of diehards, the hard core of various cryonic companies that have been fighting for years for the recognition of vitrification by the American government.

Cryonic companies specialise in freezing the heads (cost: $100,000) or bodies (cost: $190,000) of deceased persons who ordered a cryograve during their lifetime. The idea behind this is that as soon as the technology is ready and robots and humans merge, sophisticated computer programs will help these people to rise from the dead and to have an eternal life. Currently, many men and women are waiting in the Sonora desert where the bodies are stored, until they are resuscitated from death.

With their mindset, the Cryos are diametrically opposed to the religious demonstrators.

As a precautionary measure, the police and a SWAT team have closed all access to the metro lines around the square.

According to our correspondent in Colorado, it is not much better at the SITCO laboratory. An incident was reported yesterday at the compound in front of the complex in which activists attacked one another and where two people were killed and three others severely wounded. The police have now locked down access to the village, only residents of Long Peaks can enter and exit.

* * *

# CHAPTER 19

## *In SITCO's laboratory - Colorado*

## *3 days earlier...*

Isabela tells us that the trial of the ALP will start the next day in New York. Since we have been completely cut off from the outside world over the last few months, we have not received much information about anything, except for the occasional words from some members of the staff.

She says that the ALP is not allowed to continue with the tests until the Court of Ethics has come to a verdict. The laboratory is therefore officially closed from this morning. Only here in the back part there is still activity going on, but the outside world does not know this.

There are reasons to believe that the trial will not be fair and that there is a chance that the ALP will be prohibited. To ensure that all the work that has been done over the past years and all the victims who have sacrificed themselves have not been for nothing, they want to continue with the tests, whatever the outcome may be.

Isabela asks if one of us is willing to continue to take the risk. Only Solenn, Indi and I are left. Albert is dead, Angelo does not want to go through the procedure again, and Nathalie is still recovering from the last test.

Isabela explains the new procedure. Our bodies will still be cooled down to a temperature of just above freezing point, but this time it will be different with the brain. Our brain will be cooled down to a temperature far below freezing point, so that it can survive longer without oxygen, which increases the chance of a very deep near-death experience.

In addition, a special chip will be placed in our brain, exactly between both eyes, as if it were a third eye. This chip will be connected to a special neuron in the brain and then linked to a special program on an advanced quantum computer. Next, there will be an upload of the person's brain to the computer, whereby the information that is currently present will be transported from the brain to the computer, so that a sort of replica of the person is created there. The chemical structure of the replica on the computer and the chemical structure of the person himself will then correspond 100% at that moment. The frequency of the atoms will be the same, which means that, at that moment, information transfer can take place between specific energy packets (photons) from the chip to the computer. It all sounds quite complicated…

As soon as we arrive at the final border during our near-death experience, we have to see how we can pass through it without losing touch with the earthly world. They do not know exactly how this will happen as there are no precedents. They do know, however, that the elastic cord that we are tied to is likely to break, which normally leads to death. They think that a specific form of observation is needed to maintain contact between the photons of the chip and those of the computer. The third eye is the director of the orchestra as it were. We will have to figure out for ourselves how to maintain this contact once we arrive there.

They fully understand if one of us does not want to take the risk. This test is not without danger. It will not be possible to intervene during the procedure. Once the brain vitrification has started, they can only follow the entire protocol. Warming up of the brain will have to take place over a period of three hours as otherwise there is a risk of ice formation in the nerve cells, and there is then no possibility of rapid warming up as they did with Nathalie ...

\* \* \*

"Who can number the sand of the sea,
and the drops of rain,
and the days of eternity?
Who can find out the height of heaven,
the breadth of the earth,
the abyss, and wisdom?
Who can search them out?"

Ecclesiasticus

"As we know, there are known knowns,
There are things we know we know.
We also know there are known unknowns,
That is to say there are some things we do not know.
But there are also unknown unknowns,
The ones we don't know we don't know."

Donald Rumsfeld

# CHAPTER 20

## 7 September 2036

New York - International Court of Ethics
Court hearing of the AfterLife Project

Transcription - Morning of Day 3

Speakers:     Antoni Riberi – Chairman of the Board
              Rosa Bernstein – Board member
              Léon Tautou – Defendant
              Jack Brigance – Defendant

A. Riberi: 'Good morning everybody. Mr Brigance, let's start with you. Do you know anything more about what is currently going on in your laboratory?'

J. Brigance: 'Unfortunately not sir. Our laboratory has now become totally inaccessible after a stab incident yesterday in front of the entrance where one of our guards was badly injured. I was able to talk to him briefly this morning. He said that, apart from him, 12 other people were present in the laboratory, including two other guards, 6 laboratory staff and medical specialists and 4 test candidates. He could not make any further statement about the activity in the laboratory itself, since he had mainly been present outside the complex to calm down the crowd. He did say that there had been quite a lot of turmoil around the complex in the past couple of days with journalists and activists coming and going.'

'As I mentioned earlier, the communication network is completely down. That is why, unfortunately I have still not been able to reach anyone, not even on the mobile network. It may be that my colleagues and the candidates are in the rear part of the laboratory, in one of the specially sealed sterile units where radiation cannot pass, and where communication is forbidden.'

A. Riberi: 'Are these perhaps the units where you normally carry out the tests?'

J. Brigance: 'Among other things, yes. There is also a closed section where all the data is stored so that hackers cannot break in, and there is a special room where the candidates reside.'

A. Riberi: 'Okay, so we still don't know for sure whether any tests are being done or not.'

J. Brigance: 'You can take my word for it that no tests are being done at this very moment.'

A. Riberi: 'The Court needs proof, Mr Brigance, not verbal assurances. We will discuss with the Board during our coffee break what kind of steps we are going to take in order to gain an insight into what is going on.'

'Mr Tautou let's continue with you for now. Please continue where you left off yesterday.'

L. Tautou: 'Thank you. Members of the Board, I told you yesterday that the individual consciousness is not only located in our brain, but that it is linked to an endless, universal consciousness outside our body, where time and space do not exist, just like in the quantum world. People who have had a near-death experience all talk about this non-locality and the omniscience.'

R. Bernstein: 'Mr Tautou, having said that, what is your opinion about the fact that in some coma patients where brain functions are no longer observed, the plug is pulled so that their organs can be used for organ donation? Doctors are convinced that the patient is dead, but the body is still functioning even though it is connected to the heart-lung machine. If, as you claim, consciousness is not only located in the brain but also elsewhere in the body, it raises the question as to whether or not this person is really dead.'

L. Tautou: 'Again, that is a very good question. People in a coma are aware of themselves and their environment, but their brain damage prevents them from communicating directly with the outside world. It is as though they are in a different world or in a different dimension at that moment.'

'There are several known cases where patients were pronounced dead because their brain functions had failed, but to everybody's surprise they woke up from their coma after a couple of months, and this was thanks to the fact that the family had refused to switch off the heart-lung machine. These patients told afterwards that they had heard everything during their coma, including the conversation between the doctor and their family in which the family was asked if they agreed to organ donation and whether the machines could be stopped. The patients could not communicate with their environment because of their comatose condition, but all of them had cried out that they were still alive and did not want to die.'

R. Bernstein: 'What you are saying now is quite horrible. It immediately raises a number of questions about the moment of death being pronounced. Apparently, people whose brain functions have stopped can still wake up?'

L. Tautou: 'Yes indeed. In 2017, scientists focused more closely on the moment at which death is pronounced. Technically, this is when the heart stops beating, and this is determined by an electroencephalogram (EEG). As soon as the heart stops, blood circulation stops, and blood is no longer pumped to the brain, which means that the brain stops functioning. The EEG then shows a flat line, and the person is pronounced dead.'

'However, in that same year, another study showed that the brain and various organs in the body can remain active for minutes to hours after the person has technically been pronounced dead.'

'Something that is not made public either is that people who have been pronounced dead and undergo surgery for organ donation are given anaesthesia because of the so-called 'Lazarus syndrome'. This is a spontaneous return of blood circulation whereby the person in question 'comes to life again' as it were. Hence the name: Lazarus (Lazarus was a Biblical figure who was raised from the dead by Jesus).'

'In addition, these 'dead' people also show visible changes in blood pressure and heartbeat during surgery when the organs are removed.'

'So, one might seriously wonder if the person in question is indeed really dead or if they are totally aware that their organs are being removed from their body one by one.'


R. Bernstein: 'Yes, I am familiar with the Lazarus syndrome. However, we end up here with a completely different ethical issue about organ donations. Could you perhaps give us a clearer idea about what exactly happens when actual death occurs?'


L. Tautou: 'Yes, well what is death exactly? When I recently asked this question to a Catholic priest, his answer was: 'I don't know because if I am here, then death is not, and if death is here, I am not'.'

'Dying and the near-death experience are very much related, one is really happening and the other just not. During a deep near-death experience, processes go on in the body which also take place with real death, but these are reversed when the person in question returns to his body, when he is brought back to life.'

'The dying process can take hours to days and is different for each person. It takes place at the level of organs up to cellular and sub-cellular levels, with each system having its own process and pace of degradation. Usually the person in question falls into a coma during the final hours.'

'As soon as the heart stops and the outside process is completed, the inner process starts. That is the invisible process of dying at a subatomic level, where the atoms become unstable and eventually fall apart to take on a new shape elsewhere.'

'In 2018, it was proven that death progresses at 2 mm per hour at cell level, in a so-called 'trigger wave'. The self-destruction of one part ignites the next part, just as with a forest fire: one tree ignites another. This process takes place simultaneously at various points in the body; as if several hot spots in the body are being destroyed at the same time.'

'The process of dying is actually a mirrored version of the process from conception to birth. Instead of everything growing and developing little by little, everything is being broken down and disappearing bit by bit.'

R. Bernstein: 'Is there still some kind of consciousness present when someone has technically died and when the body is cold?'

L. Tautou: 'Although it is rare, there are reported cases of people who woke up after spending a few days in the mortuary.'

'In one of her books, Phyllis Atwater describes the near-death experience of the George Rodonaia from Russia who suffered a car accident in 1976, for which the KGB was found to be guilty. Since it was a politically charged death, an autopsy was decided upon after three days. When the man was lying on the autopsy table and they started to make the first incision, he suddenly started to shake. He said later that during his near-death experience, he was suddenly pulled back into his body, which turned out to be at exactly the same time that a knife started to open him up. He was immediately transferred to a hospital where he underwent a recovery period of nine months. This man lived for years afterwards.'

R. Bernstein: 'This actually corresponds to the story of the Lazarus syndrome that you just mentioned. These are rather sinister but apparently real possible scenarios.'

L. Tautou: 'Indeed.'

R. Bernstein: 'You also mentioned a kind of comatose situation that happens during the actual dying process. Is this the same type of coma as the one that a person can fall into after a car accident, for example?'

L. Tautou: 'No, a coma after a traffic accident is a very different type of coma than the one during the dying process. A coma due to a traffic accident involves brain damage caused by heavy trauma, but recovery is still possible. In a coma during the actual process of death, organs and cells deteriorate and stop functioning one by one, and there is no possibility of waking up.'

R. Bernstein: 'Would you compare a coma experience to a near-death experience?'

L. Tautou: 'No. A coma is not a near-death experience but a phenomenon in itself. You could see it as a state where the individual consciousness is turned inwards, in which the person travels, as it were, in their own psyche. During a near-death experience, on the other hand, one makes contact with an external consciousness in a dimension of existence outside one's own psyche. The latter also happens during the dying process.'

R. Bernstein: 'And what about deathbed visions?'

L. Tautou: 'A deathbed vision is an interesting phenomenon that also stands on its own. It is not a near-death experience. It occurs just before or during the effective death. The dying person predominantly sees deceased relatives and friends, and sometimes also spiritual beings who have 'come to fetch him'. Heavenly songs and music might be heard, and they see a heavenly paradise where they will go after death.'

'These visions occur without the patient losing consciousness. They find themselves in two worlds at the same time. On the one hand, they observe 'the other side', while on the other hand they are still anchored in their earthly body in the material world and can report on what they experience.'

'To explain this further, I would like to remind you of the story told by my colleague Kurt Susskind about the clocks from grandmother's day that start ticking at the same time because they have the same vibration frequency.'

'When people are nearly dead, the molecules slowly drift apart. The frequency of the photons (energy particles) changes. Their vibrations slowly start corresponding to the vibrations of the next world. These people can see what happens after death.'

'People who have such a deathbed vision are usually free from fear of death at that moment. They usually face the end of their life very happily. We will get back to this later.'

R. Bernstein: 'You say that, during a near-death experience, communication can take place with loved ones who have already died. What is your opinion about telepathy, and people who say that they can communicate with spirits in other worlds?'

L. Tautou: 'Telepathy can be seen as communication without using the five senses, or as the art of being connected to a different kind of vibration.'

'People who have had a near-death experience are much more sensitive to perceiving these vibrations after their experience. But people who have never had a near-death experience may also have this high degree of sensitivity. Consider, for example, cases where people suddenly 'receive' a message that something has happened to a relative who lives far away, or that a family member is in danger.'

'We are talking about a sixth sense here; our intuition. Indigenous tribes such as Indians or Aboriginals, for example, have a well-developed intuition. In Western culture, logic has prevailed and children are taught from an early age that anything beyond order and logic is not or cannot be true. That is why there are only very few people in our Western society who actually have this gift.'

R. Bernstein: 'Another question Mr Tautou. We have often talked about human free will in recent decades. What do people who have had a near-death experience say about this? Is everything predetermined or do we have a say in things and decide ourselves what happens?'

L. Tautou: 'These people report that everything happens according to the previously discussed cause-and-effect pattern; something that we cannot oversee with our limited consciousness. The famous philosopher Spinoza once put it very aptly: 'Suppose you take a stone and throw it away. And halfway, you give that stone a conscious and a rational brain. That little stone will then think it has free will and will explain to you rationally why it has decided to take the route it has now taken'.'

'Our consciousness gives eloquent, usually very plausible explanations about what we do. But this is purely an illusion. Brain scientist Benjamin Libet showed in his experiments in the 1970s that the body already shows a reaction before the brain 'decides' to take action.'

'People feel that they have a free choice, but that is just pure ignorance.'

'Another illusion is that we think we are in control and we are the ones who make the rules. This applies to everything we do in our daily lives. But when we look at the human body for example, we see that almost everything happening inside is beyond our control. Our heart ticks automatically, digestion is automatic, we breathe automatically, nerve impulses are automatically coordinated; even when we are asleep, all these processes continue.'

'We want everything to happen the way we want it and when it suits us, but unfortunately it doesn't work that way in the universe.'

R. Bernstein: 'It is sometimes said that the key to life is the gift of letting go.'

L. Tautou: 'And that is very true. There is a well-known story from Ramesh Balsekar who expresses this particularly well:

'Man first creates his God and then he prays to him. Then he expects God not only to answer his prayers, but he also wants them to be answered exactly as he pleases. For example, there was a man who was walking around on a mountain. He slipped, fell and just managed to hold onto the edge of the abyss. As he was hanging there, he called to heaven: 'Is there anyone up there?' There was no answer. Then he really started praying. 'Is there someone up there who can help me, please?' Then there was an answer: 'Yes, I will help you, but then you must do exactly what I say.' The man said, 'Yes, yes. I will do everything you say.' The voice said, 'Let go.' There was silence. One second, and another one. Then the man asked: 'Is there anyone else up there?'

R. Bernstein: 'So you say that free will and being in control are ideas that we create ourselves and see as the truth, while this is in fact not the case?'

L. Tautou: 'Exactly. Near-death experiences clearly show this. We have no control whatsoever over what happens to us in the coming seconds, minutes, hours or days, or what happens in our surroundings. Events are unravelling, and we do not know why they take place there and then.'

'In fact, we are no more than a small consciousness with a personality that experiences life through a body. The only thing we can do is accept it as it is and watch what happens along the way.'

R. Bernstein: 'Okay. Let us concentrate on some of the other elements you mentioned which occur during a near-death experience.'

A. Riberi: 'I suggest that we do so after a coffee break, colleague Bernstein. Let's resume in half an hour.'

* * *

# CHAPTER 21

*In SITCO's laboratory - Colorado*

*3 days earlier... in the evening*

That evening, the three of us are sitting in the living room, which looks a bit more spacious now that the others are no longer there. We are on standby; we can be called at any minute. Or not. It depends on what happens in New York. If the verdict is positive, they will probably wait until everybody has returned, otherwise we will be hearing it shortly.

Solenn and Indi have been in a deep discussion for some time now. Both wonder if they want to continue, especially now that the next test includes the vitrification of the brain. Indi believes that the near-death experience she had has given her a good idea of what it looks like on the other side and she doesn't really feel the need to go any further. Solenn is interested but does not feel in the best shape physically.

She asks Indi: 'What are your thoughts about death? Why are most people so afraid of it? Death can also be a liberation for someone who has had a long illness. Why do people who are terminally ill often choose to continue with harsh medical treatment that may extend their lives a little bit, but usually at the expense of the quality of life? Why do we try to stretch out life and postpone death at any cost? Is it fear? Is it ignorance? Are those negative ideas about death actually true?'

Indi looks at her and says: 'In my opinion, dying is only a transition to another state of being. Many people are scared to death of dying; there is some kind of taboo about it, whereas it is actually the only certainty we have during our life. We do not know what will happen tomorrow, or next year, but we do know that we will die at some point. It is the fear of the unknown, the loss of control that we think we have that holds us in its grasp.'

Solenn nods my way and says, 'Yes, Robin suggested something like that this week, that fear is one of the biggest illusions there is.'

'Yes, that is true,' replies Indi, 'I think the more you identify yourself with your limited body and ego, the bigger the fear of death will be. If you realise that your ego is not your true self but a created illusion, then it all becomes less dramatic right away. Do you know the story in the Bible of that rich man who goes to Jesus?'

Solenn shakes her head.

'That rich man,' continues Indi, 'tells Jesus that he has lived according to the ten commandments during his entire life and now wants to be even closer to God. He asks Jesus how to do that. Jesus answers: 'Give all your possessions away and follow me'. But it was impossible for the man to give up his earthly belongings, and he left with a bowed head. Jesus then told his disciples the following parable: 'The chance of a camel crawling through the eye of a needle is greater than that a rich man enters the Kingdom of God'.'

'What does that mean?' Solenn asks.

'It basically says that people who are very materialistic and fully identified with their image and ego will have the most difficulties at the time of their death. They will know the greatest fear as they cannot let go of their earthly possessions and their cultivated image. They want to stay alive at all costs. But since this is not possible and because they are being pushed to the new world by death, they start to resist fiercely because they feel that they are losing control.'

Solenn nods: 'Nice story; it fits in well with our current materialistic society. I think that the fear of death is also so intense because many people think that everything will stop afterwards. And that inspires fear, doesn't it? A great deal of fear. Isn't it true that you have learned about the ancient ways of thinking, Indi, and that they all say that death is not the end?'

'Yes indeed. Everything transforms but never dies. Energy never ends. It only changes form. Look, for example, at the life cycle of a drop of water: it evaporates, the vapour becomes a cloud that turns into rain, and out of the rain another water drop is formed, which evaporates again. It is a continuous repetitive cycle. The same happens with our essence, our energy. It has always been there and will always be. In the East, people talk about life energy. In India they call it 'prana', in Japan it is known as 'ki' and in China they refer to it as 'chi'. Many religions view this life energy as a person or a being outside ourselves, a divine power or appearance such as God, Allah,

Jesus, Krishna, Shiva or Buddha. In the spiritual world, this energy is seen more as a part of man himself.'

Solenn picks up her glass of water and says: 'I wonder to what extent we actually know our real nature. I think we live in some kind of a dream in our daily lives, far from reality. I remember one of William Shakespeare's quotes. He said that the world is a play, and people are only actors. People come on stage, play their role and then disappear again.'

Indi rolls her wheelchair to the small kitchen and returns with a bag of peanuts.

'The Toltecas in Mexico already said thousands of years ago that we live in a dream. A dream created by our parents, by the environment we grow up in and by religion. As soon as we are about five or six years old, we lose contact with who we really are. From that moment on, our ego is formed by the external world, and our connection with the universal network is broken. We are actually stuck in a system that is difficult to get out of. As we grow up, we are placed in certain boxes, and we cannot really avoid following the rules, norms and values that are imposed by society.'

'Yes', says Solenn, 'We always want to do everything that is in our power to be accepted by everyone and to be part of society, don't we?'

'Yes indeed', answers Indi, 'and that is at the expense of our authenticity, our intuition. If we want to get in touch with the universal network again, we have to go back to how we used to be as a child, back to our creativity, back to our intuition.'

Solenn takes a handful of peanuts: 'We are lucky we have been able to relive this connection during our near-death experience.'

Indi nods: 'Before I got MS I travelled quite a bit. I went to Mexico to stay with the descendants of the Aztecs and Toltecan people and I spent three months with the Indians. These groups experience this being one with the universe in their daily lives. They live a simple life and are in constant contact with nature, something that we lost a long time ago here in the West.'

She picks up a piece of paper and a pen and starts to draw: 'Look, you know what the evolution of man looks like, right? In all the books it is represented by five or six images, the left image being a monkey, which then slowly changes until the picture on the right takes the form of a human being walking upright. But if you take a good look at it, there should actually be a few more pictures on the right-hand side where the human being gets thinner and thinner until finally a straight vertical line is formed which is then repeated in different thicknesses with a number on top. A barcode, as it were. Over the years, we have actually become no more than a number in the system, herd animals that have become increasingly distant from reality through individualisation, money, power and status.'

She sits back in her wheelchair again: 'During my near-death experience, I felt that we are part of something far bigger, and that there is no such thing as a separate self. I don't know what will happen with the vitrification test, but if there is a new near-death experience where you can cross the border, it will certainly be spectacular.'

Solenn yawns and stands up: 'I really don't know whether I should participate or not. I think that if I manage to cross the border, it might well be that I no longer want to come back to life here. What is your opinion Robin?'

***

"We are programmed entities,
Consciousness wrote the script,
Consciousness is the producer,
Consciousness plays all the roles in this drama,
Consciousness experiences joy and pain
through the instruments called 'human beings'.
Because the scenario has already been written,
nothing else will happen than
the unwinding of the film
and the only thing we can do is sit back and witness."

Ramesh Balkesar

"Death is not the opposite of life.
Life has no opposite.
The opposite of death is birth.
Life is eternal."

Eckhart Tolle

# CHAPTER 22

## 7 September 2036

New York - International Court of Ethics
Court hearing of the AfterLife Project

Transcription - Morning of Day 3 - continued

Speakers:     Antoni Riberi – Chairman of the Board
              Rosa Bernstein – Board member
              Yannis Cohn – Board member
              Léon Tautou – Defendant

A. Riberi: 'Welcome back. After a short deliberation, we, as members of the Board, have decided to instruct the police to search your laboratory first thing tomorrow morning to determine whether there is any activity going on.'

'Colleague Bernstein, you said before the break that you had a few more questions about other issues that occur during a near-death experience?'

R. Bernstein: 'Yes indeed. Mr Tautou, you were talking about a border where the person realises that once they cross the line, they cannot return to the body. Could you explain this any further?'

L. Tautou: 'This border is often experienced by people who have a deep near-death experience. At the border, they are held back by a sort of elastic string. Behind them, they see the tunnel they just came from, and in front of them they see a border. Here they are told that it is not yet their time and that they must go back. At that moment, they feel that it is only this thin thread that connects them to earthly life. If that thread breaks, then they 'go over'.'

R. Bernstein: 'Earlier on, you also mentioned omniscience; why do these people no longer possess this ability when they return to their earthly bodies?'

L. Tautou: 'Raymond Moody says in his books that there seems to be a basic rule in all near-death experiences which states that the knowledge acquired from the afterlife must be forgotten upon returning to earthly life.'

'It may be that we are not supposed to have this universal knowledge here on earth, or perhaps it is the ultimate goal of every human to somehow learn to connect to it during our lives.'

'It may also be that this knowledge is incomprehensible to contemporary man and that it would lead to total chaos. Compare it to the people who lived a few hundred years ago. If we were able to travel back in time and we had told them about cars, washing machines, telephones, the Internet or drones at the time, what would have happened? They would probably have declared us crazy and would have burned us at the stake.'

'Another possibility is the limited capacity of our brain, which simply cannot handle this large amount of knowledge. If you imagine that, as mentioned earlier, we are connected to universal consciousness like little puppets, then you can imagine that these thin connecting strings can only pick up some of the knowledge; there is just no more capacity.'

'What happens during a near-death experience is that a change in vibration causes the thin string between the individual consciousness and universal consciousness to disappear, as a result of which universal knowledge is available to the person in its entirety. Upon return to the body, the string is recovered and the knowledge shrinks again to the daily limited version.'

R. Bernstein: 'Okay, I understand. I have another question for you. Are there people who have been told during their near-death experience why death also affects children? Is there perhaps a certain logic in the time span that an individual is here on earth?'

L. Tautou: 'Yes well, why do some forms of life exist longer than others? To be able to answer this to some extent, we must briefly return to the atoms and molecules of my colleague Kurt Susskind. He told us that atoms are incredibly small and that they have vibrating strings. If we now look at the animal world, we see that very small single-celled organisms already consist of billions of atoms. Now a certain amount of energy per second is needed to keep an organism alive. This smallest single-cell bacterium does not weigh more than one billionth of a gram, and needs one tenth of a billion watts to stay alive. But the largest animal on earth, the blue whale, which weighs more than 100,000 kg, needs a few hundred watts to stay alive.'

'So, why is it that many bacteria only live for an hour but a whale can live for more than a hundred years, while the former uses very little energy and the latter a lot?'

'Well, the answer to this is that it has something to do with the blueprint that can be found in everyone's DNA.'

'As you know, DNA is the genetic blueprint that everyone receives at birth, a mix of 23 maternal and 23 paternal chromosomes. This blueprint is a kind of long thin lace of 2 metres and can be found in every cell of every living creature.'

'Our candidates say that the length of time that we stay here on earth is determined in advance in this blueprint, and that this has everything to do with the cause-and-effect pattern that has already been discussed.'

R. Bernstein: 'Right. To be honest, it is still not entirely clear to me, but let's go on to something else. What does the near-death experience say about reincarnation?'

L. Tautou: 'Some people who have had a near-death experience say that they not only saw an overview of their own lives but also experienced previous lives, although in a different way. They perceived globally where they had lived, when and with whom, but personal characteristics were missing. One of our candidates, a modern Jewish female rabbi, said the following after her near-death experience, and I quote: 'Reincarnation exists. I met young and old souls there. Young souls have not been reborn that often, they still have a lot to learn. Here on earth we sometimes see people who already have a great life wisdom at a young age and who act as adults when they are still young teenagers. These are old souls that have been reincarnated many times.'

'A few decades ago, a large-scale investigation was conducted into reincarnation by psychiatrist Ian Stevenson, from which amazing things emerged. I can heartily recommend his book to you.'

R. Bernstein: 'Thank you Mr Tautou.'

'Do people change after a near-death experience?'

L. Tautou: 'Most of them change enormously after this experience. They obtain a completely different view of what is really important in life and no longer fear death because they know that death is not the end. They have experienced that our soul (our individual consciousness) remains after physical death and that we merge with an infinite or universal consciousness afterwards.'

'They feel a great connection to everything. That is why they also call their experience 'an experience of oneness'. Love for oneself, for others and for nature become the most important things in life. Other things become unimportant, for example everything that is temporary or has a material aspect, such as having a lot of money, a big house or an expensive car. They have learned that life is a gift, and that life really only wants to be lived in the most cheerful and intense way possible.'

'However, a small percentage of people indicate that the experience did not make them any happier. Loneliness, being misunderstood by their families and friends and partner loss (divorces) were mentioned as the cause.'

'As I mentioned earlier, many have greater intuition after this experience. There is also an increase in spiritual feelings. However, interest in organised religion diminishes.

'Another interesting thing to report is that just after their experience, some people feel that their bodies have brought back cosmic energy. Devices in the house break or go crazy, watches no longer work, lamps explode. These people have been in direct connection with other vibrations, and when they are back on earth these vibrations apparently only break down slowly.'

R. Bernstein: 'Can you explain why there is still so much resistance to the near-death experience?'

L. Tautou: 'There is resistance among doctors and scientists in particular. In their disciplines, something can only be believed if it can be explained and if it can be proven. As long as that is not the case, they say it is philosophy. Medical practitioners learn from day one that everything can be explained and that mystical experiences are invented tales. We hope that with our research we can create an opening for discussion where we will move away from these old-fashioned views.'

R. Bernstein: 'Various religions suggest that only human beings can go to heaven because they are the only species on earth with a consciousness. What does the near-death experience say about this?'

L. Tautou: 'Studies especially of children who have had a near-death experience contradict this entirely. After leaving their body and meeting with the being of light or with other creatures, children often (and more often than adults) meet with their deceased pet.'

R. Bernstein: 'These same religions often preach about heaven and hell; that we must pay for our earthly sins when we die. Is something said about this by these people?'

L. Tautou: 'As I explained earlier, it is the individual who acts as a judge during the near-death experience and who makes a judgment about his own life. The person experiences the consequences of his actions emotionally. The essence of light only radiates acceptance and love.'

'There are, of course, negative near-death experiences that might be thought of as hell. But as you have already heard, this often concerns suicide attempts in which the person in question is made aware that this is not the right way of doing things.'

'The stories about hell and having to do penance after our death come purely from religious indoctrination.'

R. Bernstein: 'Thank you Mr Tautou, I don't have any further questions at this moment.'

A. Riberi: 'Good, then I suggest .....'

Y. Cohn: 'I am sorry to interrupt, colleague Riberi, but may I ask the defendant some other questions related to this subject?'

A. Riberi: 'Of course, colleague Cohn, please go ahead.'

Y. Cohn: 'Mr Tautou, you say that hell and the fact that we have to do penance after our death only comes from religious indoctrination. What do you base this conclusion on?'

L. Tautou: 'Hell does not exist. It is a phenomenon that was created thousands of years ago by a number of powerful leaders so that humanity would do exactly what they were told to do; so that each individual would follow the herd as a sheep. Unfortunately, almost all religious movements still preach that hell exists. This hell is seen as a terrible place where people who 'behaved badly' during their life on earth will go, as well as those who are not part of the 'right religion'.

'I would like to add a footnote and tell you about an interview that recently appeared in the media. In this interview, a prominent Baptist minister and a Protestant pastor both claimed that Muslims belonged to the wrong religion, Islam, and therefore would not go to heaven. A Catholic nun added that Atheists should think twice before rejecting God, otherwise they would not be admitted either ... ... All these statements are completely unfounded fairy tales that can lead to great anger among the groups addressed.'

'According to our candidates, we all become neutral beings after death. All our individual particularities such as differences in religion or culture are eliminated. The light, the omniscience, the universal consciousness, the 'All' as some call it, with which we will be reunited after death, is only love and goodness.'

Y. Cohn: 'Then why is it that ever since the first human being lived on this planet, almost everybody believes in some God?'

L. Tautou: 'Because religion used to have an evolutionary advantage.'

'Before there were any laws, groups were kept together by imposing strict guidelines and rituals that people had to follow. In the last century, many new religious movements have emerged, and more than 43% of wars have been instigated out of religious causes.

'Where religion used to hold groups together, it now separates people and creates division.'

Y. Cohn: 'But the vast majority of people on earth still participate in one of the main religious movements.'

L. Tautou: 'That is not entirely true. The number of Agnostics and Atheists is growing rapidly, and within the main religions we see other movements developing, such as Mysticism in Christianity, Sufism in Islam, the Advaita Vedanta in Hinduism and the Kabbalah in Judaism. These movements have more to do with spirituality and emphasise awareness and inner transformation.'

'And to be honest, that is much more in line with how people feel after a near-death experience.'

'Even scientists become part of these side movements. Niels Bohr turned to Taoism, and we all know that Einstein was a mystic.'

Y. Cohn: 'So you really think that if humanity were to think differently about religion, the world would look very different?'

L. Tautou: 'Yes, I truly believe so. How many times in history has God's name been misused to justify the most terrible crimes?'

'Beautiful things could happen if people were more open to other ideas and if they took their own religion with a pinch of salt. For example, contraception could be used in Africa and South America, the number of AIDS patients would decrease; children would no longer die unnecessarily from infectious diseases because vaccinations would be permitted again, and albinos would no longer be slaughtered in Africa because we know that the devil does not exist. The list is long...'

A. Riberi: 'Okay, let us leave this subject for now. I propose that we have a lunch break and resume at 2 p.m.'

* * *

# CHAPTER 23

*In SITCO's laboratory - Colorado*

*3 days earlier... in the evening*

R obin?', Solenn asks again, 'What is your opinion? Do you want to undergo the vitrification test?'

I look at her and say: 'You know, I have experienced a few things lately that are so bizarre that they really triggered my curiosity about a possible universal energy, a hereafter, a heaven or whatever you want to call it.'

'For example, sometimes I only feel energy moving back and forth in my body, but my body itself is completely numb, as if it doesn't exist. It is a very strange feeling and it reinforces my idea that everything around us and we ourselves are nothing more than pure energy.'

'There have been some occasions in the past couple of years where I looked death in the eye and had visions that seemed incredibly real. The first time was when I dreamed I was driving in my car at night on the way home. When I arrived at the top of a hill, I suddenly saw that if I were to die at that very moment, I would step through the asphalt in one hundredth of a second. The asphalt would change from its horizontal position to a vertical position, and I would just step through it as if it were some kind of fabric. Compare it to a film in the cinema where the actors suddenly step out of the screen...'

'...After that, I would end up in some sort of space (say the cinema room), where my own life film would still be projected onto the screen, but with which I could no longer make contact because there would be no possibility of stepping back into the screen. (By the way, this can be compared to our near-death experiences: we can still see the people on earth but we can no longer make contact with them). After leaving this interspace or cinema room (after real death), another world opens up where all people and all beings reside who had already crossed this border earlier on.'

'Shortly after this, I had another vision in which I came eye to eye with death. It was during a dream in which I knew I was dreaming and could observe what happened; a lucid dream as it were.'

'On a market square in an old village on top of a hill, a large white truck approaches me at high speed, the driver brakes hard but the truck crashes into the side of my small white car. Just before the crash happens, time stops and a slow motion picture starts. I step out of my body and, from that moment on, I observe everything from above. Everything happens like a film, slide after slide.'

'I was given a preview of what would happen in the next hundredths of seconds: I would try to climb out of the car and run off before the big collision occurred, but I would not be fast enough.'

'I saw that, as the truck got closer, I would not make it, that the impact would be too great to survive. From above I experienced this as fine, except that I would like to continue to take care of my dog.'

'At the moment that I was thinking about my dog, I came back into my body and understood that there was no other solution. I felt that the heat caused by the impact was so high that my essence could not do anything else but switch to the next screen, to the next film, to the next world. When I realised that, I felt that it was okay, I understood that someone else would take care of my dog ...'

'After these visions, I had another lucid dream in which it seemed as though I was linked to the universal knowledge. I suddenly understood a Slavic language and I noticed that I did not comprehend the actual words but understood what was being said. When I woke up, all this knowledge disappeared like snow before the sun ...'

'I experienced the same during my near-death experience, says Indi, 'The beings I met did not speak as such, but everybody understood each other. It seems as though there is a universal language that is completely different from the spoken word. And just as you say, all knowledge disappeared when I woke up.'

'I would like to know what the truth is,' I continue, 'Are we sleeping here and do we really wake up after death, or is this earthly life the real life and is there nothing after death? Imagine if the vitrification test really offers the possibility of finding out more ... wouldn't we be the pioneers on this journey? Doesn't someone always have to be the first? Someone has to tell humanity what the truth is after having been to the other side...'

# FRACTAL – Bridge to the other side

\* \* \*

"Seeing the world in a grain of sand
and a heaven in a wild flower,
Hold infinity in the palm of your hand
and eternity in an hour"

William Blake

"After silence that which comes nearest
to expressing the inexpressible is music"

Aldous Huxley

"Dance like nobody is watching,
Love like you never have been hurt,
Sing like no one is listening,
And live like it is heaven on earth"

Rumi

# CHAPTER 24

## 7 September 2036

New York - International Court of Ethics

Court hearing of the AfterLife Project


Transcription - Afternoon of Day 3


Speakers:    Antoni Riberi – Chairman of the Board

Léon Tautou – Defendant

Kurt Susskind - Defendant


A. Riberi: 'Welcome back. I believe that we have come to the end of your explanation about the near-death experience, is that right Mr Tautou?'

L. Tautou: 'Yes that is correct.'

A. Riberi: 'Right, then I assume you will now give us information about the research itself?'

L. Tautou: 'Not yet, sir. I would first like to give you an overview of the links between the near-death experience and natural science at the universal and quantum levels. This is precisely what it is all about and what we said at the beginning of this hearing: thanks to the combination of these various disciplines, it has been possible to find answers to many questions about death and what happens after death.'

A. Riberi: 'Alright, yes I remember you stating this, please proceed.'

L. Tautou: 'First of all we can report that people who have a deep near-death experience feel vibrations and warmth at the start of the experience when body and soul are separated.'

'In the quantum world, this means that, at that moment, our physical body becomes unstable at a subatomic level and photons (energy particles) are released.'

'As you know, one of the laws of nature, the 'Law of Conservation of Energy', says that energy is never lost.'

'Well, in other words, this means that the energy released in the form of photons at the start of a near-death experience ultimately forms our astral body.'

'It is important to mention here that the degree of trauma (moderate or heavy) determines what the astral body will look like. In the case of severe trauma, people feel that they are reduced to a small dot, while in moderate trauma, where fewer atoms in the body have become unstable, there is still a body that is perceived as a kind of misty copy of their own physical body. The number of photons released apparently depends on the gravity of the trauma; the heavier the trauma, the more photons are released and the deeper the near-death experience (because after all, there is more 'fuel'). And the more energy is released, the more vibrations are being felt.'

'Then, after stepping out of the physical body, an expanded consciousness, an all-knowingness – omniscience – is experienced; all knowledge is present at once.'

'We can say here that, at that moment, the individual consciousness shifts to the universal consciousness. The string that attaches the earthly body to the universal consciousness and that only allows a small amount of knowledge to pass through is now disconnected, so that the entire range of knowledge becomes available at once.'

'One can suddenly be in a different place, even on the other side of the world, just by thinking about it.'

'As you now know, this is called non-locality in the quantum world. Photons can influence each other at great distances, at hundreds of kilometres, as has been proven on the Canary Islands and between the satellites and the Earth.'

'Time and space no longer exist.'

'Then follows the tunnel, through which they travel very quickly, faster than the speed of light. In a few seconds one can travel through many solar systems.'

'Here we can say that the tunnel is a so-called 'wormhole' and forms the connection between the two worlds: the earth and the hereafter.'

'It is perhaps interesting to mention here that the famous Dutch painter Hieronymus Bosch already made this link in the 15th century. One of his paintings shows a tunnel with light at the end and several persons walking towards this light. This painting is part of 'Visions from the hereafter' and is called 'Ascension to Heaven'.'

'After the tunnel, a horizon or border is experienced, a point of no return, the border of death.'

'We can say here that this border is the event horizon of a black hole.'

'One feels at this point that one is still attached to the earthly body with a kind of elastic.'

'This elastic can be explained as a string from the quantum world: the small vibrating energy packages that make up our entire universe.'

'At this border, one feels that, if the string breaks, one will step into the black hole, attracted by the white light in the distance. This is, by the way, also mentioned in the Old Testament of the Bible in the book of Ecclesiastes: 'Remember your Creator (...) before the silver cord is removed (...) before the dust returns to the earth and the spirit returns to God .... '.'

A. Riberi: 'Mr Tautou, sorry to interrupt you, but your colleague Mr Brigance said that everything that ends up in a black hole is pulled apart. How is it then possible that after our death we can travel through a black hole?'

L. Tautou: 'Until recently, it was indeed assumed that everything that ends up in a black hole would be pulled apart due to gravity. The famous astrophysicist Stephen Hawking was one of the pioneers who challenged this theory. He was convinced that photons could travel through black holes without being pulled apart.'

'And he turned out to be right. Our research shows that this is indeed possible. Two of our candidates who had a deep near-death experience and who were reduced to photons were indeed able to travel far into the black hole until they reached the small point in the middle.'

'Arriving at this point in the middle, the chaos of vibrations, was so tremendous that continuing would automatically have meant the cord they were attached to would break.'

'Both candidates experienced explosions at this point and saw a white light behind a huge screen of chaos, but were then drawn back into their own bodies.'

A. Riberi: 'What kind of explosions are you talking about?'

L. Tautou: 'The explosions in the middle of the funnel are caused by the collision of a black and a white hole, as my colleague Brigance explained before.'

'These explosions are gamma flashes that occur as a result of the collision of particles with their antiparticles.'

A. Riberi: 'Okay. To continue this line of questioning, in one of your colleague's documents I read that this same Stephen Hawking looked for a way to make black holes disappear or to allow them to evaporate. Now, if I understand correctly, according to you and your colleagues, black holes indeed disappear or evaporate because of collisions that occur between certain matter and antimatter?'

L. Tautou: 'Yes indeed.'

A. Riberi: Then please explain the following: if each one of us, all those 7 billion people, have to travel through a black hole to the hereafter after our death, where on heaven's earth are all those black holes then? We only know of one black hole, the one that is in the centre of our galaxy, don't we?'

K. Susskind: 'If I may answer to this question Your Honour?'

A. Riberi: 'Go ahead, Mr Susskind.'

K. Susskind: 'Black holes not only exist at a universal level, but also, and more so, at a nano level or quantum level. During my plea, I told you about the small quantum particle, the string that moves around us, in us and even through us. There are open and closed strings. The closed strings float freely through space and can move from one dimension to another (such as the gravitational particle 'graviton', for example).'

'Now, take the 27 kilometre-long tube from CERN in Switzerland and visualise a collision between two particles. After the collision, a closed string disappears from the tube. This means that so much energy is released at the moment of the collision that a passage (a wormhole) is formed through which the closed string can travel and thus disappear.'

'Well, this is exactly what happens after we die. Just before death occurs, our essence changes into photons, into a small dot. These photons travel through a tunnel (wormhole), and end up at the event horizon (black hole). As soon as real death occurs, these photons collide with their counterpart (antimatter), causing an explosion (at that moment they are at the smallest point of the black hole, the singularity). This is the moment of real death. After the explosion, they end up on the other side (the white hole), where anti-gravity forces them out into the other dimension.'

'Now, these black holes and wormholes are everywhere in the dark energy around us. They pop up and disappear one after the other. The explosions they cause are invisible to our eyes because they occur in black holes, and as you know light cannot escape from there.'

'So… we know that they are there, but at this moment we cannot measure them because we do not (yet) know how to do that.'

'Another important detail is that all these black holes that are present all around us at quantum level, are in turn linked to larger black holes, which in turn are linked to the black hole in our galaxy, which is connected to the black hole in its cluster of galaxies, which in turn is linked to a black hole in its super cluster, et cetera. It looks like a Russian matryoshka doll, you know this set of wooden dolls of decreasing size which are placed one inside another. They are all the same and all linked to each other, but just diminish in size.'

A. Riberi: 'Thank you for this clarifying explanation Mr Susskind'.

'Now, let me return to you Mr Tautou.'

'Earlier on, one of your colleagues talked about empty space and dark energy. He said, among other things, that vibrations were observed in the dark energy below the point of zero and that you would tell us more about it?'

L. Tautou: 'Yes, indeed. During one of our final tests, the candidates were kept in a cooled state for a longer time. Because of this, they had an even deeper near-death experience. The two people I just mentioned indeed observed this dark energy.'

'This energy is located between our world and the other dimension, at the end of the funnel in the black hole and goes beyond the point of absolute zero.'

'These two candidates mentioned that they saw other forms as themselves releasing the string, and stepping through a thin vibrating energy layer. When they saw this layer up close it turned out not to be dark but to consist of particles that were so incredibly small, with a vibration frequency that was so high, that they were only noticeable from very close by. One of them told us, and I quote: 'I just knew that this was the final fusion process between the universal and myself. It was as though these incredible small particles were floating in and around me to form a unity with my own essence, which appeared to consist of these same particles'.'

'Apparently, we are not only talking about magnetic vibrations here, but also about invisible moving electrical wires that create some kind of spider web that covers everything in the universe, and which can be found all around and through us.'

'These two candidates also said that this vibrating layer of energy is holographic, meaning that it is a 3-dimensional image on a 2-dimensional surface. They could see the other side (the white hole) but could not go through this layer without actually dying.'

A. Riberi: 'Can you explain the word holographic?'

L. Tautou: 'The holographic principle can be found at universe level, but also in quantum physics and even in our consciousness. Do you know what a hologram is?'

A. Riberi: 'Yes, but please explain again.'

L. Tautou: 'A hologram is a picture that appears to be 3-dimensional if you look at it from different angles. You can find them on our passports and on banknotes, for example. The most important feature is that the stored information is present everywhere on the picture, meaning that if you were to cut the picture into small pieces, each piece would show the entire picture. The smaller it gets the fewer details it will show, but it would still be the same.'

'The famous physicist David Bohm developed a model that describes the universe itself as a kind of hologram. According to him, the universe 'unfolds', spreads in its entirety, within a kind of cosmic medium. Every single piece in the universe (every star, every planet, but also every person, every tree, and every grain of sand) reflects the whole.'

'It may not be easy to understand, but it is very similar to the aforementioned cobwebs or to the road networks that lie above one another, which become bigger and bigger and which are intertwined or connected via roundabouts.'

A. Riberi: 'Okay. Please continue.'

L. Tautou: 'To continue with the links between the near-death experience and the quantum world, we also see a clear similarity when we look at the notion of time.'

'Time is a very special phenomenon that only we can experience as such. It is something that humans themselves introduced thousands of years ago. From waking up in the morning to falling asleep at night, we are totally conditioned by time.'

'A week has 7 days, a year has 365 days and the moon revolves around the earth in 28 days. The alarm clock rings at a precise time in the morning, at work we have to appear at a certain time, an appointment is scheduled for a specific time, and an average human life lasts around 700,000 hours.'

'Our life is totally dominated by time, which greatly limits our sense of freedom. People who have had a near-death experience say that they entered a dimension where time no longer exists, where past, present and future coincide, and where everything happens simultaneously, just like in the quantum world.'

'We, as earthly beings, cannot experience this fusion of time because otherwise everything would happen at once.'

A. Riberi: 'So, in other words, the phenomenon of time is something that man himself has created in order to function better in daily life?'

L. Tautou: 'Yes, exactly. The timeline that, according to Einstein, runs from left to right across the dimension chart, can only be experienced at the moment itself, in the present.'

'We cannot experience other places on this line during our earthly existence. Apparently, this will only be possible when we move on to another dimension, when we die. Which is, by the way, actually quite logical because otherwise we could change the past, for example. And according to the laws of nature, changing something that runs from the past to the present on this earthly timeline is totally impossible as otherwise the so-called 'grandfather paradox' would occur, which says that if you go back in time and murder your grandfather, it would be impossible for you to retell it because you would not exist.'

A. Riberi: 'I see...'

'In the quantum world, there are more of such paradoxes I believe? If I correctly understand the additional documentation that we have received, it is possible to be alive and dead at the same time according to the scientist Schrödinger, with his famous cat experiment in the box?'

L. Tautou: 'Yes, that is true. According to the Copenhagen interpretation, Schrödinger's cat is simultaneously dead and alive until a measurement or observation takes place. As said, the quantum world is very complex and sometimes totally incomprehensible. Niels Bohr once said: 'If you haven't been shocked by quantum mechanics, it means that you have not understood it'.'

'If you want more details about the above paradoxes, please ask my colleague Susskind. He can explain it better than I.'

A. Riberi: 'Thank you for your clarification, I don't think additional details are necessary for now. I propose that we take a short break. You are all kindly requested to be back in this room in half an hour.'

\* \* \*

# CHAPTER 25

## *In SITCO's laboratory - Colorado*

## *At that same moment...*

Isabela is restlessly pacing back and forth through the laboratory. The blue sapphire on her finger has been vibrating for a few minutes now. Then suddenly a screen pops up on one of the walls and a message from Jack appears:

--- Isa, there is a great deal of doubt in New York. There is one silent jury member, and we do not trust Cohn. We are not sure about Riberi either. We have decided to resort to plan B. Put everything in motion and inform the candidates. Tomorrow morning, the police will be coming to search the laboratory. Make sure that 12 employees are visibly present at the front area. Two reliable colleagues from Léon will join you tonight, Alex d'Houzé and Emily Stutton. Emily is a cardiologist and fully familiar with all the procedures, Alex is the Swiss brain behind G..... Start the procedure as soon as you can ...---

\* \* \*

"I see how the world slowly turns in a desert,
I hear the loud thunder that will kill us,
I feel the suffering of millions of people,
And yet when I look up to the sky,
I think that everything will be fine,
Because even this harshness will cease,
There will be peace and quiet again in this world"

Anne Frank

"Stars are merely musical notes,
Heaven is the score,
Human beings are the instruments"

Christian Morgenstern

# CHAPTER 26

## 7 September 2036

New York - International Court of Ethics
Court hearing of the AfterLife Project


<u>Transcription - Afternoon of Day 3 - continued</u>

<u>Speakers:</u>    Antoni Riberi – Chairman of the Board

Jon Bennett – Board member

Léon Tautou – Defendant

Kurt Susskind - Defendant


A. Riberi: 'Mr Tautou, before the break you outlined the similarities between near-death experiences and natural science at a universal and quantum level. Please continue.'

L. Tautou: 'Thank you, Your Honour.'

'I would like to show you one final similarity, namely that of the aforementioned vibrations and their mutual frequencies.'

A. Riberi: 'The floor is yours, Mr Tautou.'

L. Tautou: 'Physicists often make the following comparison regarding different wave frequencies. They say that our living rooms are filled with hundreds of radio signals from all over the world, but the receiver of the radio is only directed towards one of them. The other signals do exist in the living room but the radio cannot pick them up at the same time because they all have different frequencies; the atoms do not vibrate in phase with each other.'

'This applies to everything around us, every single thing and every living being has its own vibration frequency. The frequencies only begin to match when death occurs.'

'People who die naturally often fall into a coma in the final phase of their lives. At this point, communication with their relatives is no longer possible. The atoms in their bodies break down little by little and gradually approach the frequency of the afterlife dimension.'

'For people who experience a deathbed vision in this final phase of deterioration, it is often still possible to communicate with their loved ones. Their stories show that, at that moment, they are partly in one world and partly in the other.'

A. Riberi: 'So, in other words, it is important that waves vibrate at the same frequency. Something that we are apparently unable to experience during our life on earth, except those who have a very high degree of intuition like the Aboriginal people you mentioned earlier?'

L. Tautou: 'Exactly, or those who end up in a coma due to heavy trauma, or those who are affected by a stroke or diseases such as dementia. Let me explain.'

'According to the most recent literature, heavy trauma causes different centres of consciousness in the brain to be switched off, as a result of which the person ends up in a coma and can no longer communicate with his environment. However, we now know that consciousness is not (only) present in the brain, right? So, what exactly happens after such a trauma?'

'When a person lapses into a coma, his consciousness ends up on a different wavelength. It is therefore no longer possible to communicate via the waking consciousness that we know here on earth.'

'One of our younger candidates told us that she had fallen into a coma a few years ago after a skiing accident. She said that she was intensely happy during her coma period. She felt as though she were dead and was fine with it. Everything felt peaceful. At the same time, she heard the stories her family told her and the music they played for her, but she could neither communicate with them nor show that she heard all their conversations. She said, and I quote: 'I could not actively participate because I felt that I was on a different frequency or wavelength; I saw them but I could not reach them'.'

'If we look at a disease such as dementia, we see that as soon as the disease really strikes, people change. Their mask falls off. It is just like with the brain haemorrhage that we have discussed before: if the left brain chamber does not function well, rational thinking, rules and norms are slowly cancelled out. People who were labelled 'cool' in their lives suddenly become friendly, those who were 'rigid' become flexible and those who were seen as sad or depressed suddenly become very joyful...'

'So... something happens in the brain that causes the left side to gradually cease and the right side (intuition) to gradually take over. The vibration of this right chamber apparently bears greater similarity to the vibration frequency of the universal consciousness than the logical left side, which is why at this point the true 'self' can better express itself.'

A. Riberi: 'Erm...okay, thanks for this clarification. I assume that your colleague Mr Greene will now take over to inform us about the research?'

J. Bennett: 'Colleague Riberi, sorry to interrupt you, but I would also like to ask Mr Tautou a question if I may?'

A. Riberi: 'Of course colleague Bennet, please go ahead.'

J. Bennett: 'Mr Tautou, during my first academic training, before turning to law (and this is many years ago), I studied the communication and survival strategy of animals. The phenomenon of vibration frequencies you talk about is also frequently evident in the animal world.'

'What is your opinion, do you think that certain animals have access to these other frequencies during their life on earth, and perhaps therefore also to other dimensions? Some animals, for example, are tuned in to the vibrations of the earth's magnetic field, such as certain bird species, aren't they?'

L. Tautou: 'The animal world is a very interesting subject, Sir, especially when we look at the differences between humans and animals. If we look at our senses and compare them to those of animals, we see that they always have one sense that is more developed than the other and that it is far more sophisticated than ours.'

'Dogs can smell far better than we can. Owls have perfect hearing. Birds of prey have such extremely well-developed eyesight that they can recognise a small prey such as a mouse from a great height. And if we take elephants, we see that in order to communicate with each other at great distances (and we are talking about many kilometres here), they make certain noises with their throats that other animals (and humans) cannot hear.'

'In addition, there are animals that have access to certain vibrations and signals that we cannot perceive. Migratory birds, sea turtles, sharks and whales, for example, are able to observe the magnetic field of the earth and use it to navigate on long journeys.'

'Bats are blind, but can find their way by making certain echo sounds to create vibratory waves that indicate where they are. The bumblebee recognises flowers from a distance by means of an electrical signal that the flower emits through its quivering hairs. And then there are animals, such as rattlesnakes, that can see heat radiation, they can track animals by observing the heat of their body.'

'So yes, it is indeed true that animals can sense certain vibrations that we cannot perceive, thanks to their sharper additional senses.'

J. Bennett: 'Yes, I do recall something of the sort.'

'Another question: I understand that in your research you use a method called 'suspended animation', and this is something that is found in the animal world. Could you explain to us exactly how this works?'

L. Tautou: 'Suspended animation, or apparent death, indeed comes from the animal world. Some animals go into hibernation, whereby their body temperature decreases so greatly that their metabolism almost completely shuts down. At that moment, it looks as though they are dead. This way, these animals can survive for months without food. They bring their entire body into a state of hypothermia (very low body temperature), where breathing and heartbeat are drastically reduced.'

'This can be applied to human beings in the same way. My colleague Robert Greene will explain this in further detail.'

R. Greene: 'Thank you Léon. Yes, members of the Board, suspended animation is a wonderful discovery. Cardiologists and neurologists have observed for decades that tissue in a state of hypothermia can survive for a longer period of time even when cell function in this tissue starts to fail. This gives doctors more time to save a seriously injured patient who has little chance of survival. Patients are put into a kind of hibernation so to speak.'

'For those of you who have never heard of the phenomenon of suspended animation, I will provide a short medical explanation:

'At normal body temperature, body cells need constant oxygen. When the heart stops, the supply of oxygen to the brain via the bloodstream also stops. Brain functions fail and the patient dies. At a very low body temperature (hypothermia), the cells require less oxygen because the chemical reactions are delayed. It takes longer for the brain functions to fail. This is what happens to animals that hibernate or, for example, to someone who survives a near-drowning death in very cold water.'

'At the beginning of this century, this method was tested on pigs. After the pigs were anaesthetised, their blood was drained extensively. Instead of blood, a cold saline solution was injected into their veins. When the pigs were cooled down to 10° C, their trauma was repaired, the salt solution was replaced with blood and they were warmed up again. The heartbeat of most pigs automatically resumed, others received an electric shock. For most of them, there was no difference between before and after the intervention and they lived as long as other pigs.'

'This method was first applied to people around 2016. It involved patients whose heart had stopped due to severe trauma. The body temperature of these patients was also reduced to 10° C. The same cold saline was injected into the aorta. For a short time, these patients no longer had any blood in their system, their breathing had stopped and there was no brain activity.'

'So technically speaking they were dead. After repairing the trauma, their blood circulation and breathing were restored, followed by the warming up of their body. Approximately half of these patients needed an electric shock to get their heart beating again.'

'A total of 162 patients received this treatment worldwide and 73 of them survived, which is approximately 45%. Consider the fact that this method was applied to people who were very badly injured. According to the statistics, the survival rate would normally have been around 7%, so this is a very positive result. Unfortunately, it was not possible at the time to apply this method on a larger scale; the cost of the required equipment was extremely high and the specialist knowledge required to put a patient under induced hypothermia was lacking in almost all hospitals.'

A. Riberi: 'Did you use this same method for your research?'

R. Greene: 'Indeed, we started our research using the abovementioned method, where the candidates were put under induced hypothermia and we reduced their body temperature to a maximum of 10° C.'

'The candidates were anaesthetized after initial cooling. Their heart was stopped with an electric shock, after which the aorta was cut open to cause rapid blood loss. This was followed by repairing the aorta, injecting the saline solution into their veins, lowering the body temperature to 10° C and connecting the candidates to the heart-lung machine.'

'To increase the chance of a near-death experience, after the injection of the saline solution we waited before connecting the candidates to the heart-lung machine. The candidates were held in this intermediate state for a period ranging between 10 to 20 minutes.'

'Of the first 900 candidates who were clinically dead for 10 minutes and whose bodies were reduced to a temperature of 10° C, an average of 30% had a near-death experience. These experiences were all incomplete for the purposes of our research. The candidates had an out-of-body experience, a journey through a tunnel, but none of them ended up at the event horizon. They were drawn back into their bodies before reaching the end of the tunnel.'

'94% of this first group returned. Here we must mention that the 54 people who died were all terminally ill patients who were in the final phase of their life.'

A. Riberi: 'Mmmm…. please continue.'

R. Greene: 'The next group of 900 were kept in a clinically dead state for 12 to 14 minutes at a body temperature of 6° C. It was striking that approximately 60% had a near-death experience. They all had a more extensive initial phase than the group before. All felt vibrations at the start of the experience and a separation of body and soul. They experienced a different way of being, without a body. Then they went through the tunnel at great speed.'

'The candidates who were clinically dead for 12 to 13 minutes came to the end of the tunnel and saw a bright light. They experienced an overview of their lives there and were then sent back.'

'The candidates who were clinically dead for 14 minutes felt they were becoming very small. When they went through the tunnel, they saw the earth from a distance and a kind of in-between world with wandering spirits. After the life overview, an evaluation and a preview of their future life followed. They all felt enormous peace. Some of them saw the event horizon in the distance, but could not reach it. They too were drawn back into the tunnel.'

'86% of this group returned.'

A. Riberi: 'What happened to the other 14%? We are talking about 126 persons if I am correct?'

R. Greene: 'That is true. The resuscitation did not work with these candidates.'

A. Riberi: 'Apart from yourself, were there any other medical specialists present who came to the same conclusion?'

R. Greene: 'At least five doctors were present during each procedure, including a cardiologist and a neurologist.'

'In all these cases, they came to the same conclusion; that death was caused by a weakened body.'

A. Riberi: 'Mmmm, and you decided to go ahead?'

R. Greene: 'Yes. Of course, we regret the fact that we were not able to bring everyone back, but this group was already in the final stage of their lives before taking this test. The candidates who died were all, without exception, terminally ill. The fact that the earthly connection with them was broken during suspended animation could be compared to passive euthanasia. Their immune system no longer functioned optimally, which caused complications after their first few minutes of apparent death, ultimately leading to their actual death.'

'Of the other 774 people who were not terminally ill, everybody returned.'

A. Riberi: '........ Continue please.'

R. Greene: 'Right, since the near-death experiences of this second group were also incomplete, we decided to bring the next group of 900 candidates into this intermediate state for one minute longer, that is 15 minutes, with a further cooling to 2° C.'

'Almost 75% of this group had a near-death experience. Almost all had a deep and intense experience similar to that of the group before, with the difference that they did arrive at the event horizon. They felt they had ended up in a kind of cortex or spiral, as it were. Some people compared it to an hourglass. All experienced this as being the absolute limit that could not be exceeded. Going beyond it would mean definitive death, and this could only happen if the elastic or cord to which they were attached were to break.'

'Of this group 73% returned.'

A. Riberi: 'And again, I assume you are going to tell us that the 27% who did not survive were terminally ill patients?'

R. Greene: 'For the most part, yes. You can find all the medical information and causes of death in the white folder in front of you. I can assure you that the entire procedure has been carried out in the same way every time and that there is no question of human error.'

A. Riberi: 'Okay. So, if I go along with your reasoning here, there are volunteers who wanted to participate in this test and who were terminally ill?'

R. Greene: 'Yes indeed.'

A. Riberi: 'Right, now, if you say that everything happens according to the law of nature and that we cannot control our destiny and cannot determine the day and time of our death ourselves, and if we do so, we will remain stuck in a grey and dark intermediate station surrounded by lost souls, then what about those volunteers who died during your research? Does it not follow that they committed suicide, or are we talking about murder here?'

R. Greene: 'I think you should look at it from the point of view of a terminally ill person. These people are given a choice between waiting for a possibly slow and painful death or participating in an experiment in which they have an opportunity to see what happens after death. Taking part will first of all give them the motivation to get through the last stage of their life with a bit more positivity; many see it as an adventure. In addition, it may offer them the option of not returning from the event horizon; in which case they face a gentler death, similar to euthanasia.'

'There is absolutely no question of murder here.'

A. Riberi: '…..You do not give a clear answer to the question regarding whether this is contrary to the laws of nature which state that suicide is not permitted, as you mentioned before.'

R. Greene: 'We explained before that no information is available from people who end their lives through euthanasia since this group always dies. What we can say is that this type of suicide does not fall into the same category as suicide committed by a healthy person. During the near-death experience of people who are terminally ill, there is apparently a possibility of releasing the cord to which they are attached in order to speed up the moment of death a little.'

A. Riberi: 'But there is no evidence of this, it is merely your assumption. It could also be the case that these people will remain in the intermediate place you spoke about earlier.'

R. Greene: 'Yes, that is indeed possible. But to give an accurate answer to this we will need to do far more research.'

A. Riberi: 'Okay, well let's continue with the research at hand first. What did you do after these three tests?'

R. Greene: 'After this third test, we did one more final test, this time with a smaller group of 55 people. We wanted to see if it would be possible to go beyond the black hole's event horizon by using the same method, but applied in a more extreme way. The bodies of these candidates were reduced to a temperature of 0.5° C for 20 minutes.'

'More than 80% of those who returned had a near-death experience. They had indeed gone a lot deeper than the groups before, and as you know there were even two candidates who went through the event horizon and reached the centre of the funnel.'

'It became clear that the longer they were in this condition, the looser the cord to which they were attached became, and the more difficult it was to return to their bodies.'

A. Riberi: 'How many people from this group survived?'

R. Greene: '36 in total.'

A. Riberi: '36 out of 55? The percentage that dies apparently increases with each test .... How many people in total died in the end?'

R. Greene: '442 to be precise.'

A. Riberi: '442 people who were killed during extreme hypothermic test experiments .... The internal documents that we have seen state that a total of 2,764 candidates have participated so far. Is that correct?'

R. Greene: 'There are a few more, we are now at a total of 2,770 persons.'

A. Riberi: 'Okay, and 442 of them died, so that is about 16% if I'm right. Correct?'

R. Greene: 'Yes, that is correct.'

A. Riberi: 'How many of these were terminally ill?'

R. Greene: 'This information can also be found in the white folder in front of you. Off the top of my head, I believe that 393 were terminally ill.'

A. Riberi: 'So that means that the other deceased candidates, 49 in total, were in good health physically? Were they all in the category of 'people with psychological problems'?'

R. Greene: 'No. We honestly never made a distinction between people with mental illnesses and physically healthy people. I know the media have talked about this, and it is unfortunate that you apparently believe this information, because it is simply incorrect.'

'All candidates are screened by a team of doctors before they are admitted to the programme. Candidates who are thought to be unstable are consistently rejected. The only classification we make is between terminally ill and healthy people.'

A. Riberi: 'Mr Greene, let me start by saying that we have not taken into account any information coming from outside. We, as judges of the Court of Ethics, are not influenced by what is put out by the media, so your allegations are unfounded here.'

R. Greene: 'Apologies, Your Honour.'

A. Riberi: 'Apologies accepted. What did the 49 healthy people die of?'

R. Greene: 'More than half of these candidates fell into a coma after the procedure, and subsequently died of cardiac arrest or other complications. And we suspect that the other half had a certain kind of choice at the border to let go of the cord.'

   'But, as we have just said, we can only find that out if you allow us to continue our research, because this requires far more very deep near-death experiences where people go beyond the event horizon of a black hole to the spot in the middle where the black hole turns into a white hole.'

A. Riberi: 'Right …...well, I propose that we leave it here for today. You will once again be escorted to your accommodation by the police. Again, I ask for discretion; there should be no contact with the press. I look forward to seeing you here again tomorrow morning at 9 a.m. and wish you all a good evening.'

* * *

# CHAPTER 27

*In SITCO's laboratory - Colorado*

*That evening....*

I t is already dark when Isabela enters our living quarters. 'The time has come', she says, 'accompany me to the lab as I have something to show you.'

As soon as we leave our living area, I see that the laboratory is no longer divided into two parts, but that a heavy iron screen has now been erected between both sides.

Isabela walks towards the iron screen and turns around: 'From the start, we have taken into account that there might be opposition and criticism with regard to our research. That is why we have chosen to build a fortified structure; a kind of a bunker. Long Peaks turned out to be the ideal place. It was possible to carve out part of the laboratory from a rock here, which could be connected to an underground tunnel that emerges above ground a few kilometres away.'

'As you have seen, your sleeping quarters and the area where the tests are being held are on the inside of the rock. An exact replica has been built on the other side, outside the rock within the (publicly) visible part of the structure. It has the same sleeping areas, a test area and a laboratory.'

'Both sections can be separated with special metal plates.'

Isabela points to the walls around us. 'To build such a special construction, we took the rock in Spitsbergen as an example, where all possible vegetables, spices and seeds from all over the world are stored.'

'The reason for this is, firstly, because our supercomputer G can only function in a radiation-free space that can be cooled to below -270° C. The inside of this rock at this altitude turned out to meet this requirement.'

'And secondly, this would be a perfect way to keep out the authorities in the event that they sought to obstruct our project.'

'There is absolutely no way to enter the rock from the outside; it is a completely protected and isolated space that can even withstand an atomic attack. Anyone entering the laboratory from outside will not see that there is a partition wall. The thick iron plates have been covered with the same stones as the rock in such a meticulous way that it resembles a continuation of the rock itself.'

Isabela turns towards us: 'As there are serious doubts about the outcome in New York, we have decided to close the doors tonight and put the separating system into operation. In the closed section inside the rock, we will start the long-discussed vitrification procedure tomorrow, a month earlier than planned. Two colleagues will join us via the secret tunnel tonight to help with the procedure.'

'For our part, we are ready. G is linked to the chips in your brain. Now it's up to you to make a decision. Who is willing to take the risk?'

We look at each other. One hand goes up ...

\* \* \*

"He who knows does not speak,
He who speaks does not know"

Lao Tse

"Look carefully, because what you will see
is not what you just saw"

Leonardo da Vinci

"For my freedom, no other limits can be found
than freedom itself;
We are not free to stop being free"

Jean Paul Sartre

# CHAPTER 28

## New York Times - 8 September 2036

Today is the fourth day of the hearing of the 'AfterLife Project' in New York. According to our source, the debate on the research itself finally started yesterday. Apparently not all the judges are on the same page. Some are purportedly biased. But is this possible in such a high court of law?

If we look at SpaceOne's Mars project, isn't it true that, thanks to the positive verdict of this same court, mankind managed to send the first man to set foot on the red planet? Should we not be more open to new inventions and allow the 'AfterLife Project' to find answers to important questions about death; answers that might benefit the whole of humanity? And shouldn't we give science the benefit of the doubt in that case?

Since yesterday, not only here in the United States but also in the rest of the world, people have been gathering on the streets. On the square in front of the United Nations Headquarters, the situation has not improved much during the past couple of hours. The number of atheists and Cryo followers has increased significantly.

At the same time, there are reports from various corners of the world from prominent church leaders who demand a ban on the project. A number of Catholic priests have travelled from Rome to New York, as well as several imams from Saudi Arabia and Iran. They have positioned themselves at the outside of the crowd, creating a great variety of different religions and non-religions. The police have their hands full keeping the crowd calm.

Derek de Bouvoire, Professor of Theology and Philosophy at Harvard University, explains in an interview with this newspaper that the separation between church and state exists in theory in many countries, but that the dominant position of the church is often still decisive when it comes to difficult and (for the church) threatening issues.

– For a summary of this interview we refer the reader to page 3. –

In Colorado, the situation seems to have calmed down now that the entire complex is hermetically sealed off. The army has positioned itself outside the complex and the protestors are now tens of metres away from the laboratory.

\* \* \*

# New York Times - 8 September 2036

## - Page 3 -

Summary of the interview with Professor of Theology and Philosophy Professor Derek de Bouvoire.

Professor Derek de Bouvoire is affiliated with Harvard University in Cambridge, Massachusetts and gives lectures on the impact of faith on society worldwide. When asked to what extent religion could influence the outcome of the 'AfterLife Project', Professor de Bouvoire gave the following outline:

'Since the beginning of time, technological revolutions have primarily pointed to one development: the emergence of a planetary civilisation. The younger generations of today are the most important ones who have ever lived on this planet; they are the ones who will determine whether we will reach this goal or whether we will drift into chaos and extermination. Science and technology have never been as important as they are today. They open up worlds that we could only have dreamt of in the past. They provide answers to life questions that we previously thought were the work of a supernatural God'.

'Since the beginning of its existence, our human species has had a tendency to believe in something or someone. Even most atheists believe in something, hence the emergence of 'somethingism', meaning an unspecified belief in an undetermined transcendent reality. Religions and sects have all developed their own commandments, doctrines, and cults throughout the ages. Due to the mutual differences, there are now more than 3,000 different religions and spiritual tendencies with a total of more than 3,000 different Gods that are being worshipped. If we look at the current 'AfterLife Project' and at the ideas about life after death in the main religions, we see that there are some similarities but also some major differences.'

'The followers of Islam, Judaism and Christianity believe, for example, in life after death and in heaven and in hell. The followers of Buddhism and Hinduism believe in the cycle of death and rebirth (reincarnation). Every movement thinks that it has a better way to serve its God through (sometimes far-reaching) rituals and customs.'

'Most of them see God as a human being, often an old and wise man with a beard. The philosopher Spinoza once said: 'That we imagine God as a human person is only because we ourselves are human beings. If a cow could speak, it would call God a Cow. And a triangle would call God a Triangle'.'

'Holding these outdated anthropomorphic views, and rigidly adhering to ancient rituals and commandments is totally obsolete in 2036. Those who still assure their followers of God's favour if they live in a certain strict way, only continue preaching that way to keep a nation or a crowd of people quiet, and it is purely based on fear. Frightening people to keep them in line is something that we have seen happening for thousands of years.'

'If we look at the individual person, we see exactly the same thing happening. People believe in heaven or in a kingdom of God out of fear. They believe in something 'that will surely come someday', in something external, in something outside of themselves. They create or invent a structure or a powerful being who is superior to themselves and who will help them during difficult moments in this earthly life. They create rituals and commandments to hold onto; something to provide a certain degree of peace and security.'

'We all know the film 'The Matrix', in which people are so primitive that they are not even aware of the fact that machines took over power a long time ago; in which people dream that they live a real life, while in reality they live in a cocoon and serve as energy for the machines.'

'Another view – slightly lesser known – is that of the sacred Akasha records – which are thousands of years old and suggest that there is a cosmic energy field in the universe, the Akashic field, where all information is stored and with which we will merge after death.'

'And let's not forget that many people believe in the existence of UFOs, that extra-terrestrial beings rule us, and that we will travel to their 'home base' after we die.'

'Just as religions preach that there is a God and heaven and hell, the aforementioned Matrix machines, Akashic records or the existence of alien colonies might very well be based on a certain truth. We just don't know.'

'This is why the research of the 'AfterLife Project' is so important. We are all in favour of technological progress on our earthly soil, so why should we draw a line where the earth ends and the mystical or divine begins? If the question of where we stand in 2036 with our faith, what is true and what is not, if there is a God or not, can be answered through technological research, I believe that the Court of Ethics should respond in favour and should not let itself be influenced by whichever religion.'

'Albert Einstein once said 'The most important thing is not to stop asking questions ... ' I think that, with the 'AfterLife Project', SITCO has found the ultimate instrument to contribute to formulating an answer as to what happens after death.'

'Let us all see the term 'God' simply as a metaphor: as something transcendent, a transcendent mystery that is all around us. And let us be in favour of technology that can turn 'believing in' into 'knowing for sure'.'

* * *

# CHAPTER 29

## 8 September 2036

New York - International Court of Ethics
Court hearing of the AfterLife Project

<u>Transcription - Morning of Day 4</u>

<u>Speakers</u>:    Antoni Riberi – Chairman of the Board

           Robert Greene – Defendant

           Léon Tautou – Defendant

A. Riberi: 'Welcome back to this fourth morning. Your laboratory is currently being searched. We will inform you as soon as there is any news. Mr Greene, please continue where you left off yesterday.'

R. Greene: 'Thank you, Your Honour.'

'I told you yesterday about one of the last tests we did.'

'When we heard from the candidates who survived that the elastic that held them to their earthly lives became weaker and weaker as time went on, we decided not to extend the time any further between administering the salt solution and connection to the heart-lung machine, and to stop at a suspended animation of 20 minutes.'

'Since these near-death experiences were not complete in terms of our research either, we had to consider other options. We started looking for a way to cool the brain even faster and to further slow down the chemical process of cell decomposition. Eventually we ended up with vitrification of the brain.'

A. Riberi: 'What do you mean by vitrification?'

R. Greene: 'You may be familiar with the term cryonism? This is a procedure whereby people who are clinically dead are 'frozen'. You have probably heard of this phenomenon, where people want to be placed in special cooling cells with liquid nitrogen after their death so that they can come back to life at a later stage as soon as the technology is ready to 'wake them up'. The bodies of these people are kept at -196° C and their body cells are filled with nitrogen.'

A. Riberi: 'Yes I am familiar with the term cryonism, it is an increasingly recurring theme in the media.'

R. Greene: 'It has indeed been discussed in the media lately, especially cryotherapy. People who undergo this therapy take nitrogen showers of -110° C to alleviate muscle pain and chronic inflammation.'

'However, that is something totally different from the cryonism that I am talking about here. With cryonism, a large proportion of the water in each cell (around 60%) is replaced with protective chemicals to ensure that no ice can form in the cells or in the veins.'

'As you know, the cooler the environment, the more slowly atoms move around. When the environment cools down in an extreme way, they move increasingly slowly until all chemical reactions finally stop at the point of vitrification. In the brain, this point is at -124° C and it takes about one hour to reach this temperature.'

A. Riberi: 'But why switch so drastically from 0.5° C to -124° C? Have any studies been carried out into the possible effect of this extreme freezing?'

R. Greene: 'As early as the last century, vitrification was applied to sperm and egg cells for 'in-vitro fertilisation'. At the time, a so-called 'slow freezing technique' was used for the sperm cells. With the egg cells, they quickly switched to a faster method, the 'fast freezing technique', by using a larger amount of freezing medium. The freezing time was then reduced from 3 hours to 10 minutes, making the chance of ice formation virtually nil.'

'In our research, we applied the 'fast freezing technique', whereby we used a freezing time of one hour.'

A. Riberi: 'Okay, but vitrification with 'in-vitro fertilisation' is something totally different from vitrification of the brain. As I said earlier, I would like to hear from you if any studies have been done at all into the effect of this extreme form of freezing?'

L. Tautou: 'If I may respond to this question, Your Honour? As this concerns colleagues of mine?'

A. Riberi: 'Please go ahead, Mr Tautou.'

L. Tautou: 'A well-known biological research centre, the 'Institute Européenne de Biopharma' in Geneva, Switzerland, has spent years investigating the freezing of animals in winter, focusing on the North American wood frog in particular. They are the ones who finally showed us the way.'

'We told you before that many animals hibernate in winter, which can be seen as suspended animation. Well, the North American wood frog is almost the only animal on earth that can freeze itself in such an extremely radical way in winter that it really appears to be dead.'

'Normally, water expands when it freezes, and this means that ice crystals will form which can damage the cells. This is, however, not the case with the wood frog. Once winter sets in, a chemical compound is released in the tissues in preparation for hibernation, and liver glycogen is converted to glucose in large quantities in response to internal ice formation. Both this chemical compound and the glucose act as cryoprotectants (as an antifreeze so to speak). This antifreeze is diffused throughout the body, and ensures that no ice crystals occur. Then the frog freezes from the outside to the inside, until finally the heart stops. 70% of its body is frozen at that point, but it is not dead. As soon as the weather warms up, it unfreezes and its heartbeat resumes.'

'This Swiss institute has put the frogs in special freezers for hours, days, months and even a few years to see what would happen to them. Not only did they find that their heart stopped beating, but also that their breathing stopped completely. As soon as the frogs were removed from the freezer and were slowly unfrozen, their hearts started beating again and their breathing resumed; even those which had been in the freezer for a few years. It is really incredible.'

A. Riberi: 'And what exactly does this have to do with your research; and once again I turn to you Mr Greene?'

R. Greene: 'Well, we have discovered that we can use this same procedure in human beings by injecting special chemicals into their brain.'

A. Riberi: 'What kind of chemicals are you talking about?'

R. Greene: 'First the substance glutaraldehyde is administered. This substance is used for the removal of warts, for example. This is followed by the injection of ethylene glycol, which is also used as coolant and antifreeze in our daily lives.'

A. Riberi: 'Isn't ethylene glycol a highly dangerous substance?'

R. Greene: 'Yes, but only if someone swallows a large quantity of it, not if injected. Children and animals are more at risk because they may like the sweet taste of this substance so much that they want to consume more, and two tablespoons are indeed fatal. In our case, there is no danger whatsoever because we administer everything intravenously.'

A. Riberi: 'Alright, please continue.'

R. Greene: 'In patients who wish to freeze their bodies for a 'rebirth' at a later stage, the body is, as we said, cooled down to -196° C. In our research, only the brain of the candidates is vitrified and reduced to a maximum temperature of -124° C.'

A. Riberi: 'Alright, and what happens next?'

R. Greene: 'After that, the process is applied in the opposite way; the brain is warmed up.'

'To do this, we use the same nanotechnology that has been deployed for the past few decades to de-vitrify kidneys, blood vessels, ovaries and livers that were frozen at -135° C.'

'In addition, our laboratory has invented an ultra-small electrical heat sensor that makes it possible to gradually bring the brain back to a normal temperature. The chips in these sensors are programmed in such a way that they diffuse heat rays for exactly three hours after implantation and then melt away automatically.'

'The entire process of vitrification of the brain takes a total of around four hours. Initially one hour to drop to -124° C and then three hours to warm up again.'

A. Riberi: 'You talk about a cooling process of one hour. But is it not true that you have to lower the temperature as quickly as possible, otherwise brain functions could be irreversibly damaged or even fail completely due to a lack of oxygen?'

R. Greene: 'Yes, that is true, but you are talking about the decrease in body temperature here and not about the temperature of the cells in the brain, which break down far more slowly. The temperature of the body must indeed be lowered rapidly.'

'In our research, we always maintain a protocol whereby the body must be cooled to 32° C within three minutes. The brain then still receives enough oxygen. As soon as the aorta is cut open and the heart stopped, we ensure that the body is brought to a temperature just above freezing point in the space of a few minutes. Only then do we start with the vitrification of the brain.'

A. Riberi: 'You just said that the fast-freezing method takes 10 minutes in sperm and egg cells. Why does it take one hour in the brain?'

R. Greene: 'Each organ is different and responds in a different way to this fast-freezing technique. It has been determined in our laboratory that there is a risk of shrinkage of the cells if the brain is frozen faster.'

A. Riberi: 'Shrinking of the brain you say? ..... '

R. Greene: 'Yes, something that we naturally do not want to happen.'

A. Riberi: 'But something that is apparently possible. If I understand correctly, vitrification of the brain has never been applied to people before, and apart from this forest frog, no further studies have ever been done to look into the dangers and possible consequences of such a procedure. That's true, isn't it?'

R. Greene: 'It is a wood frog, not a forest frog. And yes, that is right. However, you must not forget that the technology has seen such an exponential growth over the past decade that the quantum computer can now exclude almost all possible risks in advance.'

A. Riberi: 'But as I understand, significant risks are still very much present, Mr Greene.'

'To be honest, from the start of this hearing I have wondered why your company did not focus your research on people who meditate, for example? They can also gain access to this other dimension, can't they? There are many Buddhist monks who, after having meditated for many years, talk about enlightenment and say that they have reached nirvana? Surely you could have focused on this group instead of applying such a radical approach?'

R. Greene: 'It is indeed possible to connect with the universal consciousness through long-term meditation. But here we are talking about very limited partial access. Something that is very different from what we see in a near-death experience, which goes much deeper and where there is total access.'

A. Riberi: 'But to start a procedure based on a method that is not proven by studies is very risky, don't you think? And of course, I am talking about the risks for the candidates in particular.'

R. Greene: 'If we were to wait for approval from the medical college, the FDA, to apply the vitrification procedure, we would be ten years on. You know as well as I do that it takes an exceedingly long time for new medicines to be introduced onto the market due to pure bureaucracy, even though they have been tested for years. As a result, hundreds of thousands of people die unnecessarily every year. You also know that, in order to circumvent this type of bureaucracy, it is important to just go ahead at a certain point and not wait any longer.'

'Having said that, it is of course important to be very sure about the matter and to use highly advanced equipment and skilled staff. The vitrification substances we use are tuned to the cells of the human brain with extreme precision. We also have a quantum computer that continuously calculates the level of movement in each cell, and it measures the temperature. As soon as even one cell deviates, an alarm goes off immediately. The computer repairs the problem straight away using special electrodes that are placed on the outside of the candidate's skull. The procedure has gone well up to now.'

A. Riberi: 'You say that the procedure has gone well so far. Does that mean that you have already applied the vitrification method to your candidates?'

R. Greene: 'Up to now we have only applied the vitrification method to special brain tissue that was grown in the lab.'

A. Riberi: 'Something very different is being said in the media.'

R. Greene: 'With all due respect sir, you are again talking about news that has been distributed on social media. As a servant of the highest court, you must know better than anyone that a great deal of this type of news is based on lies.'

A. Riberi: 'Mr Greene, I do not appreciate your tone and I believe you are now crossing the line with your comments for the second time. If this happens a third time, you will be fined for contempt of court, and you may be detained until the end of this trial if a fourth instance occurs. Is that clear?'

R. Greene: 'Yes, Your Honour.'

A. Riberi: 'I hereby suspend the hearing for half an hour so that we may all withdraw for a moment. We will resume at 11 a.m.'

* * *

# CHAPTER 30

*In SITCO's laboratory – Colorado*
*In the back part of the rock,*

*That same day at 8.40 a.m. ...*

Total silence....The screen on the wall show that the police have been pulled out in large numbers. The laboratory has been turned completely upside down. Heaps of paper are scattered across the floor, drawers have been pulled open, chairs are lying on their side, and computers and other electronic equipment have been confiscated.

*11.50 a.m. ...*

The laboratory is quiet and peaceful again, the dust has settled. Everyone has left, except for the six who are still in the back section inside the rock: a cardiologist, a computer expert, the head of the medical staff and three candidates ... one of whom is currently undergoing the ultimate vitrification test.

They started off well, first the vitrification of the brain, then the slow warming up. The heat sensors have done their job efficiently and so far, no swelling has occurred.

The temperature of the brain is now at -104° C, more than two hours after the start of the procedure. Robin's heart is not beating on its own, but is regulated by the heart-lung machine.

Minutes pass by. The heart monitor and the computer seem to coincide in terms of sound; the ticking and bleeping is slowly matching. A good sign.

Apart from the ticking of both machines, it is very quiet in the laboratory. Everyone is waiting. Then the computer suddenly starts rattling.

'We are in contact,' Alex shouts. A large series of zeros and ones appears on the screen. In the middle, an image unfolds, moving outwards and repeating itself continuously. Isabela is dumbfounded. The Fractal. What exactly did Kurt say about the fractal during the last meeting? With a swipe from left to right on an invisible screen on the wall, she opens a document, the recording of the meeting. She scrolls forward until Kurt's face comes into the picture.

'A fractal is a geometric figure in which the same pattern is repeated again and again on an increasingly smaller scale. This repetition continues when zooming in at the level of molecules, and right down to the string level. Because the patterns repeat themselves endlessly on an ever-smaller scale, one of their characteristics is that they are infinite; there is no end.'

'There are many fractals in nature. A tree, for example, with its large branches on which smaller side branches grow, on which little twigs grow. Or the leaf of a fern, or a snowflake that grows very slowly and where each part always looks the same; or a flash of lightning in the sky.'

'The interesting thing is that the human body also consists of all kinds of fractals. You can see our brain and all its connections as a kind of super network of roads running above each other and through each other. Or take the 100 billion nerve cells that are all connected to each other; or our lungs with their bronchi, bronchioles and vesicles, resembling a tree with increasingly smaller branches; or our vascular system. They all have the same kind of pattern that is repeated down to the smallest details.'

'In addition, these very patterns can also be found on a cosmic level: stars are connected like a web to form galaxies together; and galaxies are linked like a web to form a star cluster; the star clusters are again connected to form a super cluster, et cetera.'

'Everything is a reflection of everything, from the universe to our blood vessels, and from our brain to the smallest atom. Think of it as a kind of Wi-Fi network, the connection fibres are everywhere ...'

Alex comes over to stand next to her. Isabela stops the recordings: 'I remember Kurt showing a snowflake on the screen that was getting bigger and bigger. It looked just like the symbol we are seeing here.'

Alex looks at the repetitive pattern on the screen and says, 'Léon told me that he hoped that once the chip was implanted in the brain and connected to G, there would be a fusion between the quantum photons in the computer and the photons in the chip in the brain of the candidate. This fusion would then form a new fractal and thus send information from one photon to another to eventually reach G...

I think that is exactly what we are seeing here, I believe you have made a major breakthrough.'

Isabela smiles: 'Yes, I think so too. That is indeed what we are seeing here. A new fractal has formed between the quantum world and ourselves. Unbelievable…'

She presses the blue sapphire and sends a message to Jack.

--- Jack, we have done it, we are in contact. It is indeed the fractal that connects both worlds. Make sure that the judges give permission, we are almost there now. ---

The fractal unfolds slowly towards the outside. It looks like an oriental mosaic piece.

Alex presses Enter, the design disappears. The cursor flashes in the top left corner of the screen. Then a new image appears, this time of birds that subtly turn into fish.

'Hey', says Isabela, 'this is one of Escher's drawings. These are the swimming fish that turn into flying birds, it is called 'Air and Water'.'

She presses Enter again. Another image appears, this time of birds turning from black into white.

'Day and Night', she continues. 'Half of the picture is during the day, with black birds flying in the sky; and the other half is at night, with white birds flying in the sky; two different worlds, but still the same. Also by Escher.'

'So that's the symbolism here,' says Alex, 'We have equipped G with all possible symbols, mathematical codes, images and sounds, knowing that the information coming from the other world would be so vast that it would be impossible to display it as such. G has therefore been given the task of acting as some sort of buffer zone, as a funnel for the information.

He types the name 'Escher' into the computer.

'Escher's drawings', he reads: 'are based on mathematical principles, on geometric patterns, on infinity; patterns that repeat themselves and then gradually change into completely different forms, but which are always connected to each other.'

Isabela looks over his shoulder and says: 'Right, now we have a fractal and two drawings of Escher ... What is Robin trying to tell us?'

The computer makes another sound and a new picture is formed on the screen. 'This is also Escher,' says Isabela, 'The Three Worlds'. It is a drawing that distinguishes three worlds: trees that shine with their branches in the water; leaves that float on the water and a fish that swims in the water.'

Alex looks at her and says: 'Let's see if we can send Robin a command from here'. That would normally also be possible, wouldn't it?'

'Yes, normally, yes.'

Alex taps on the question mark symbol and presses Enter. The cursor flashes in the top left corner of the screen. No reaction.

Then suddenly a deafening choral song is emitted from the speakers.....

\* \* \*

"The breezes at dawn have secrets to tell you
Don't go back to sleep!
You must ask for what you really want.
Don't go back to sleep!
People are going back and forth
across the doorsill where the two worlds touch,
The door is round and open
Don't go back to sleep!"

Rumi

"Break free from conformity
Live beyond the normal"

Anonymous

"We must be willing to let go of the life we planned
so as to have the life that is waiting for us"

Joseph Campbel

# CHAPTER 31

## 8 September 2036

New York - International Court of Ethics

Court hearing of the AfterLife Project

Transcription - Morning of Day 4 continued

Speakers:    Antoni Riberi – Chairman of the Board

Yannis Cohn – Board member

Robert Greene – Defendant

Kurt Susskind – Defendant

A. Riberi: 'Welcome back.'

'Mr Greene before the break you told us that you applied the vitrification method to special brain tissue that you grow in your laboratory?'

R. Greene: 'That is right, Your Honour.'

A. Riberi: 'Please explain in further detail.'

R. Greene: 'We did not apply it to any old piece of brain tissue, but to various life-sized artificial brains.'

'As you know, human brains are being made with real blood vessels in various laboratories worldwide. This method started some 18 years ago and in recent years it has resulted in 'mini' brains of about 700 grams with their own astrocytes, nerve cells, synapses and everything else that is present in our own brain.'

'Well, we have continued the development of these mini-brains in our laboratory for the past year to develop a full-size brain that totally resembles our own. They now have a similar weight of around 1.4 kg.'

'It is on these artificial brains that we have tested the vitrification method.'

A. Riberi: 'And how did these tests go?'

R. Greene: 'They went pretty well.'

A. Riberi: 'There were no complications?'

R. Greene': 'During the test phase, we noticed that absolutely no problems occurred during the freezing process itself.'

'The warming up from -124° C to + 37° C in a time span of three hours also progressed in a normal way; the brain tissue recovered entirely as it should.'

'Only in a few cases did cerebral oedema (brain swelling) occur during the warming up.'

A. Riberi: 'Isn't that extremely dangerous?'

R. Greene: 'Yes, it can indeed be dangerous, but we had anticipated this risk to some extent.'

'Cerebral oedema can occur when an excess of heat is released, which causes the brain to swell. Most of our candidates apparently return to their body at the moment they are linked to the heart-lung machine during the warming up process. The returning energy (the photons in their brain) gives a sudden extra warming, which could then cause this swelling.'

'To avoid this problem in the future, we will adjust the heat sensors slightly differently. Where they first provided a pre-programmed constant heating up of 161° C (from -124° C to +37° C) in exactly three hours, we will now adjust them so that in the event of a sudden warming up in their environment, they will slow down their own heating time.'

'In addition, as a precaution, four holes will be drilled into the candidate's skull so that the brain can expand a little bit.'

A. Riberi: 'How can you be so sure the brain will recover and the memory of the candidates will not be affected during such a radical procedure?'

R. Greene: 'Let me start by saying that most of our memory is not located in the brain but in 'the cloud', as you have already heard from my colleague Léon Tautou.'

'In addition, the brain is very flexible and can fully recover even after severe trauma. As mentioned earlier, sometimes people are resuscitated for up to 45 minutes. During that time, it seems as though the brain is in a kind of standby mode. Many of those who regain consciousness afterwards do not suffer any neurological injury.'

'We do the same here. The brain of the candidate is held in a standby condition for four hours during the vitrification process, after which it is reactivated.'

A. Riberi: 'And how does this reactivation work?'

R. Greene: 'By warming up, followed by electrical stimulation.'

A. Riberi: 'Do you mean an electric shock?'

R. Greene: 'It is actually a combination of an electric shock and a specific activation program supplied by our quantum computer.'

A. Riberi: 'I did not know that today's quantum computers also provide programs that can resuscitate someone from a clinical death?'

R. Greene: 'Not all of them can. However, ours is a very unique type that is indeed equipped with such a revolutionary program.'

A. Riberi: 'Can you tell us more about it?'

R. Greene: 'To better understand the technology of our supercomputer, it might be useful if I first tell you more about the quantum computer itself.'

A. Riberi: 'I think we all have a good understanding of what a quantum computer is and does nowadays, but please go ahead.'

R. Greene: 'Well, to go back to the basic principles, a normal binary computer calculates with bits, as you know. A quantum computer is capable of making extraordinary calculations thanks to bits with quantum properties, the so-called qubits. Qubits are small particles in superposition, they can have the value 0 and 1 at the same time, while with a normal binary computer the value is either 0 or 1. Each qubit doubles the number of possible outcomes. With 10 qubits, there are 1,000 possibilities, with 20 there are 1 million possibilities and with 30 there are 1 billion possibilities. 50 qubits offer roughly the computing power of the binary super computers we had in the years 2018-2020.'

A. Riberi: 'I believe this is the capacity of most of today's quantum computers, isn't it?'

R. Greene: 'No, most of the common quantum computers have a maximum capacity of 100 qubits, double the power of 2018-2020.'

A. Riberi: 'Ah okay, and yours has even more capacity?'

R. Greene: 'Indeed. Our quantum computer has a capacity of no less than 200 qubits, and can therefore give as many outcomes as there are molecules in the universe. The capacity is enormous. There are currently only four of these types in the world.'

A. Riberi: 'Amazing.'

R. Greene: 'Yes, it is quite revolutionary indeed.'

A. Riberi: 'Continue please.'

R. Greene: 'One of the aspects of the quantum computer is its sensitivity. The environment can disturb the quantum properties of the qubits and cause errors in the calculations, even with the slightest movement. This is why a very stable and sterile environment is required.'

'Another aspect is that the small qubit particles must be cooled to below -270° C with liquid helium. To achieve this, a special room is required where radiation cannot penetrate. Radiation-free areas of this kind are very scarce worldwide and are usually set up by governments in secret locations.'

'We were lucky that, thanks to our collaboration with the Biopharma Institute in Geneva in Switzerland, the Geneva canton allowed us to create a special space in our laboratory where the quantum computer G they designed could be stored. Our setting meets both requirements, a stable and sterile area which could be cooled down to almost the point of absolute zero.'

A. Riberi: 'Okay, and Swiss engineers are in place to work on it?'

R. Greene: 'From the start, our technicians and those in Switzerland have been working together. They have equipped G with the most advanced self-learning algorithms, making her smarter and smarter every day.'

A. Riberi: 'Are you saying your computer is so smart it has developed this activation program that you just talked about on its own?'

R. Greene: 'Yes. We sometimes had to give directions with regard to some specific formulas but for the most part that is indeed what happened.'

A. Riberi: 'Alright, but how does this computer connect with your candidates?'

R. Greene: 'Our laboratory has developed a special microscopically small nano-chip, the TP-5. Simply put, this chip connects the quantum computer on the one hand and the candidate on the other. The chip is placed in the brain, in the hypophysis of the candidate, which is linked to the rosehip neuron on the outside of the brain, just above the right ear to be precise. This enables teleportation to occur when being linked to G.'

A. Riberi: 'Why in the hypophysis and in the rosehip neuron?'

R. Greene: 'Do you recall that 98% of all cells in our body are replaced every few months, except for some cells in our brain and eyes?'

A. Riberi: 'That is what your colleague told us yes.'

R. Greene: 'Right, well, the hypophysis and the rosehip neuron are just about the only areas in the brain where there is no cell renewal. And consequently, the ideal place to put the chip.'

A. Riberi: 'And what do you mean by teleportation?'

R. Greene: 'Teleportation is the direct transfer of a person from one place to another without the person physically moving. In other words, the person disappears in one place, to reappear in another place at exactly the same time. Just like what happens in the quantum world. You remember that particles can disappear somewhere and reappear instantaneously somewhere else?'

A. Riberi: 'Yes.'

R. Greene: 'Well, in our case the chip ensures that a copy of the entire candidate is sent to our quantum computer G. As soon as the candidate has a very deep near-death experience, so many photons are released that they provide enough energy to influence the photons between the candidate, the chip and G, so that information can be transferred. Just like what happens with the photons in the quantum world.'

A. Riberi: 'I don't exactly understand what you mean. Can you explain further please?

R. Greene: 'It is what my colleague Kurt Susskind told you three days ago. Quantum entanglement connects particles across any distance. The basic idea behind it is that two particles can be linked to each other – that is, affect each other's quantum states – over any distance, even if that distance is the diameter of the universe.'

'In this case we talk about a connection between photons here on earth and photons on 'the other side', which transfer information between each other.'

A. Riberi: 'Okay, I see.'

R. Greene 'This information will then be sent encrypted from the chip to G. And G has learned to pass on this information to us through symbols, which our experts in turn, have learned to decipher.'

A. Riberi: 'So if I understand correctly, this chip creates a kind of bridge between the candidate and the quantum computer?

R. Greene: 'That's right.'

A. Riberi: 'And you are under the impression that you will receive the information you are looking for through this channel?'

R. Greene: 'Yes indeed. Information transfer will take place as soon as the candidate releases the elastic cord to which he is attached at the event horizon of the black hole; when passing over to the other side.'

'As you know, this is the very moment that an explosion takes place between the black hole and the white hole which provides a big boost of energy. It is also the moment when real death usually occurs.'

A. Riberi: 'Suppose that this indeed works, what is the likelihood that the candidates will return healthy and alive? You and your colleagues have said yourselves that real death occurs at the moment when the explosion takes place. After all, the cord is broken at that moment?'

R. Greene: 'Yes, that's right, but as you know, according to quantum theory, it is also true that two photons on the same vibration frequency will remain connected to each other.'

'In our case, this is a specific computer frequency, between the chip in the candidate and his uploaded version in G. Two different objects, but both with photons that are on the same frequency. So even when the cord is broken, the link between the person and G should still exist as long as observation takes place.'

A. Riberi: 'I am starting to lose you here Mr Greene. Are you saying that the chip and the computer remain in communication even though the cord is broken?'

R. Greene: 'Yes indeed. As you know, consciousness is connected to the body. Body and brain act as a conduit or channel to pass the information through. When the body and brain are dead, the chip is still connected to G, which continues to process information. The chip receives information from the candidate from the other side, from the universal consciousness, and transfers it to our computer G. Information transfer is therefore still taking place.'

A. Riberi: 'Okay, let me go along with your line of reasoning for a minute. So, you say that the person in question can send information through the chip to the computer, and that the computer can then subsequently decode the information?'

R. Greene: 'Yes, that is what it comes down to.'

A. Riberi: 'Right. But how do they return to their life on earth?'

R. Greene: 'The candidates' return to their bodies with the vitrification method differs from the return during a normal near-death experience. Since the individual consciousness has crossed the border and the elastic cord has been broken, they will not be able to return on their own. At any rate, they will have to be resuscitated, hence the electrical shock that will be applied at the same time as G's special activation program. As soon as the heart ticks again, the expectation is that the return will occur at the same point in the rosehip neuron via the hypophysis because this is where the chip is located.'

'The energy of the incoming photons will reconnect via this chip and will make new connections (synapses) with the neurons in the rest of the brain and then with the rest of the body ....'

'However, we are not 100% sure that it will happen exactly this way. The candidates will have to discover for themselves how to find their way back. They may communicate with us at that moment and tell us what we can do from our side to help them. We just don't know exactly what will happen because it has never been done before.'

'Technologically speaking, it is all possible, however.'

A. Riberi: 'But at a very high risk.'

R. Greene: 'Yes and no. As we said before, technology has made such incredible leaps forward that the present quantum computers, and especially those such as G, can monitor almost anything if supplied with the right programs.'

'The candidates are properly informed of the risks in advance. Of course, they are all given the choice as to whether or not they want to start the procedure.'

'We actually offer the same kind of trip that was offered to the candidates of SpaceOne a few years ago. It could be a one-way trip; no one has ever gone to this place before and therefore no one has ever returned. But who knows, maybe they will be the first to succeed and go down in the history books as being the first humans to set foot in the hereafter and return safely back to earth.'

A. Riberi: 'But there is a high risk that it is a one-way trip.'

R. Greene: 'Unfortunately, we cannot give you a percentage or success rate because this will be the first time; it has not been done before. SpaceOne was also unable to give you figures at the time, but the Court did decide in their favour, in the interest of science, remember? We hope you will do the same here. We are currently just a hair's breadth away from an incredible scientific breakthrough. And as I just said, technology is on our side.'

A. Riberi: 'It is true that SpaceOne did indeed get the green light then, but we are talking about many more victims here.'

K. Susskind: 'If I may respond to this Your Honour?

A. Riberi: 'Go ahead, Mr Susskind.'

K. Susskind: 'I think it is important to reiterate to the Court that our research has already made various discoveries that have helped science advance.'

'For example, look at our two candidates who went through the event horizon. That is an absolute breakthrough. We now know there are even smaller particles, particles that are smaller than strings, that vibrate in their own way at a very high frequency level. We also know that dark energy is buzzing with activity and lies in another dimension that we can only access after death or during a near-death experience.'

'Furthermore, we now also know that it is consciousness that creates reality. That particles only get a specific shape when observed by a spectator. And that it is actually our individual consciousness that causes the collapse of the wave function, the process in which the countless possible outcomes of a measurement suddenly change into just one. This is all new material for physicists worldwide to investigate further.'

'There are bound to be more breakthroughs if we continue with our research. By giving us permission to proceed and thus informing citizens worldwide what happens after death, you could be partly responsible for positive changes in society.'

'There will be more solidarity, intuition will receive more attention, and very importantly: religious tensions will subside. Wars might become a thing of the past if we know whether or not there is a God.'

A. Riberi: 'Thank you for your explanation, Mr Susskind. I assure you that we will look into the issue and examine your pleas carefully. I propose that we leave it here for now...'

Y. Cohn: 'Colleague Riberi, sorry to interrupt, but I would like to comment on what the defendant just said and ask him some further questions?'

A. Riberi: 'That is fine. But I suggest that you do that after our lunch break.'

Y. Cohn: 'Okay.'

A. Riberi: 'I suspend this morning's session and ask you all to be back in this room at 2 p.m.

***

# CHAPTER 32

*In SITCO's laboratory – Colorado*
*In the back part of the rock,*

*That same day 12.15 p.m. ...*

The sound that comes out of the speakers is deafening. Alex and Isabela both shrink back.

'That is one of the first passages from the St. Matthew Passion', says Indi, who is moving towards them from the other side of the laboratory.

Isabela looks at the screen: 'Okay, so we now have three drawings by Escher, a fractal and the St. Matthew Passion. Which of you has an idea what this means?'

Alex frowns and says: 'I don't think we should take it literally. It is not about Escher's drawings or about Bach's compositions. Since G works with symbols and numbers, we should probably do the same: approach the information symbolically. We have birds here, simultaneous worlds and Bach. Somewhere between these three there is a link ...'

The music stops, the cursor flashes again in the top left corner of the screen. The soft tick of G slowly starts to match the heart monitor's bleep.

Silence in the laboratory. Solenn comes up from the bedroom and joins the group. Everyone is lost in thought.

## *12.40 p.m. ...*

'Something has suddenly occurred to me', says Indi: 'There is a famous writer who describes the world metaphorically. This might point to him. His best-known work is called 'The Illusions of Bach'.'

'Hence the music of Bach', says Isabela.

'Yes', continues Indi: 'and one of the stories is about a seagull.'

'Escher's birds', says Isabela.

'Exactly.'

'It doesn't mean anything to me, what is it about?'

'It's about a seagull named Jonathan', Indi continues:

"Jonathan is rejected by the group because he sees flying not only as a functional tool but as something challenging, and views it as a life goal to learn as many tricks as possible. After being rejected by the group, he learns what it is like to live not as a follower, as a seagull among thousands of others, but to be free. He learns to become stronger by being the exception, and in his perfection, he finally manages to master the top levels of flying. Eventually he returns to the flight of seagulls and chooses to help the others with what he has learned."

'What does Robin want to illustrate with that?', asks Isabela.

'I think we should first look at the other drawing by Escher, Indi continues: 'The three worlds'. I think it illustrates one of the other works from the 'Illusions of Bach'. It is one of his best-known stories called 'The stream in the river'. It is about the freedom of a water creature who decides to move into the wide world.'

'A water creature?' Solenn asks.

'The fish in Escher's drawing?' Isabela suggests.

'Yes, that is what I think,' Indi replies: 'Do you know the story?'

Isabela, Alex and Solenn look at each other and shake their heads.

'It is an interesting story,' continues Indi: 'and it is especially known in Eastern philosophy. It goes like this:

"Once a village of creatures lived at the bottom of a crystal-clear river. The current of the river swept silently over all of them – young and old, rich and poor, good and evil – the current going its own way, knowing only its own crystal self.

Each creature in its own manner clung tightly to the twigs and rocks at the river bottom, for clinging was their way of life, and resisting the current was what each had learned from birth.

But one creature said at last, 'I am tired of clinging. Though I cannot see it with my eyes, I trust that the current knows where it is going. I shall let go, and let it take me where it will. If I keep clinging, I shall die of boredom.'

The other creatures laughed and said, 'Fool! If you let go, that current will tumble you in all directions and smash you against the rocks, and you will die more quickly than boredom!'

But this one did not feel any fear, and taking a deep breath let go, and at once was tumbled and smashed by the current across the rocks. But just in time, as the creature refused to cling again, the current lifted him free from the bottom, and he was not bruised and hurt any longer.

And the creatures downstream, to whom he was a stranger, cried, 'See, a miracle! A creature like ourselves, yet he flies! See the Messiah has come!'

And the one carried by the current said, 'I am no more a Messiah than you. The river is very happy to set us free, if only we dare to let go. Our true work is this journey, this adventure.'

But they cried even more 'Saviour!' while clinging to the rocks. And when they looked again, he was gone, and they were left alone making up legends of a saviour."


'Alright,' says Isabela, who is getting signals from Emily from the other side of the laboratory that extra blood is needed for Robin. 'What does Bach mean by that, or rather, what does Robin mean by that?'


Indi continues: 'Both stories are metaphors to transmit the philosophy of freedom. The deeper meaning is that one must let go in order to live real life. Not hold on tightly to rituals and a self-created image, to the control that we think we have, to the system in which we live. Not like zombies following the leaders, but choosing one's own way. As long as we are identified with our own created ego, we will continue to think we are in control of life and that the 'I' is something very different from the 'he' or 'she', that we are all separate entities. As soon as we see that the mind is playing a game with us, that everything is based on illusions and that we have no control whatsoever, we come to a different state of being. Only then can we see the real world.'

'As the water creature tells its fellow creatures that their essential work is that journey, that adventure; this also applies to us. The purpose of every human life is to gain experience in the most conscious state as possible, without the narrow limits that are imposed by others. Completion of this process during earthly life is the achievement of perfection ...'

'Typical Robin', says Solenn.

'Why?', asks Alex.

'Robin has a strong ideological aversion to blindly following the group, or the system if you like, to pursuing rigid protocols and strict guidelines that put people in boxes.'

'That is a whole lot of philosophy,' says Isabela, while giving Emily two extra units of blood, 'but I think the most important thing now is to get Robin back. His situation seems to have become unstable, and I don't like the look of it at all.'

* * *

"The meaning of life is just to be alive.
It is so plain and so obvious and so simple.
And yet, everybody rushes around in
a great panic as if it were necessary
to achieve something beyond themselves"

Alan W. Watts

"A great man keeps the spirit of a child"

Lao Tse

"Every child is an artist;
The problem is to remain one
once we grow up"

Pablo Picasso

# CHAPTER 33

## 8 September 2036

New York - International Court of Ethics
Court hearing of the AfterLife Project

Transcription - Afternoon of Day 4

Speakers:    Antoni Riberi – Chairman of the Board
             Yannis Cohn – Board member
             Hanna Linstrøm – Board member
             Kurt Susskind – Defendant
             Léon Tautou – Defendant

A. Riberi: 'Welcome back.'

'Colleague Cohn, you said before the lunch break that you had some more questions for Mr Tautou?'

Y. Cohn: 'Yes indeed.'

'Mr Tautou, you said that if we find more answers to important life questions, there will be more solidarity, intuition will receive greater attention, religious tensions will subside and wars might become a thing of the past. Don't you think that you paint a euphoric and a somewhat childishly imaginary picture of reality here?'

L. Tautou: 'What is reality? In this neurotic Instagram world in which we currently live, we think that we, as very little creatures, have a lot to say. We believe we have so much power that we can even make climate and nature adapt to our guidelines. But let's take a rational look at the facts Mr Cohn. The universe is more than 90 billion light years in diameter. Somewhere in that huge space with trillions of stars there is a galaxy called the Milky Way. In this huge galaxy of 100,000 light years in diameter, there is a small blue planet at the top right-hand corner, which we call Earth and which races through space at around 67,000 miles per hour. And on that little planet Earth, 7 billion very little creatures are swarming around who think what they do is very important. Do you see the absurdity?'

'It is indeed true that people are becoming smarter and that technology is making huge leaps forward. However, our intelligence is actually very limited. We have no idea how some of the things work. Look, for example, at our brain or our DNA. Or take the cause-and-effect pattern of all our words and actions ... we just have no idea about the how or the why.'

'We have to become aware of this again, to see ourselves for what we really are, to regain modesty. Because even though we achieve technological heights, we basically know very little.'

Y. Cohn: 'You paint quite a negative image of our knowledge here, don't you think?'

L. Tautou: 'It is not my intention to paint a grim or negative picture. I am just trying to explain that we can change things in our society through our research.'

Y. Cohn: 'Solidarity and intuition. Why should we go back to intuition? It is mainly thanks to our rational mind that we have made such major advances in the past decades.'

L. Tautou: 'Going back to intuition is very important. Do you remember my argument two days ago in which I told you what thoughts actually are?'

Y. Cohn: 'Yes.'

L. Tautou: 'Many of us here in the West live in our heads; we identify ourselves with our thoughts, as if we are one with them. Because of this, we have lost contact with our body. And that's a shame.'
    'As the monks, and all those who practice meditation, show, the unity between body and mind is very important. And not least for our personal well-being.'
    'When we are sick, we can heal much faster by making contact with our body. How do we know this and how does this process work?'

'Well, everything revolves around energy. Energy that flows all around us and through us. As soon as we live purely in our heads, fluid movement of the energy from top to bottom is no longer possible. Barriers are created by our thoughts. All energy stays in our head because of all that thinking.'

'As you know the brain's main task is to think and to find solutions to issues. And believe me, that takes a lot of energy!'

'Because of all that energy consumption in our upper chamber (or in the 'head office' as we call it sometimes), there is no longer enough energy available, for example, to heal a sick body or to fight a virus from within the body.'

'That's why the return to intuition is so important. To restore the unity between body and mind.'

Y. Cohn: 'Those are your words, Mr Tautou. We live in a world of information. Thanks to our rational thinking and our smart brain, we now thrive so well here.'

L. Tautou: 'We live indeed in a world of information; you are right about that. And the amount of information doubles every two years. But it is not our brain that is smart, that is where you are wrong. Apparently, you still see our brain as the hard disk of a computer, but it is only a channel for all the information to pass through; information that is stored around us in 'the cloud'.'

'And fortunately so, because how could this brain of 1.4 kg handle a doubling of information every two years, while having a maximum capacity and while not growing along with the exponential advance of technology? Just think about that!'

Y. Cohn: 'A difference of opinion, Mr Tautou. Let me ask you something else. A couple of days ago, you talked about the cells in our body. You said that almost 100% of cells are replaced by new ones over and over again. Isn't that true?'

L. Tautou: 'Yes that is right.'

Y. Cohn: 'Okay, now, you also suggest that consciousness is located somewhere other than in the brain. Correct?'

L. Tautou: 'Yes that is correct.'

Y. Cohn: 'Right. Now, if we then put one and one together, then you are actually saying that we do not exist. Isn't that right?'

L. Tautou: 'You are saying that very jokingly, with all due respect Sir.'

Y. Cohn: 'Jokingly or not, that's what you think it comes down to, isn't it? We have a body, which you think is a self-renewing envelope; we have a personality which, according to you, is nothing other than an ego created by the brain; and a consciousness that is outside of our body. So, then my question to you is, Mr Tautou: who the hell are we?'

L. Tautou: 'I see that it makes you laugh, but you are probably closer to the truth than you think or than you want to be.'

'As you have heard before, our personality consists of several layers. Buddha once compared it to an onion, you can peel it off layer by layer to the inside where it is empty. The outer shell is our ego, further inward is the waking consciousness and subconsciousness, eventually culminating in pure essence.'

'In the near-death experience we see that the personality of a person (their ego) dies when the person dies. What remains is their essence. And what exactly is this essence?'

'That is precisely this universal consciousness that we have been talking about these past few days; this vibrating energy, the inside of the onion.'

Y. Cohn: 'Mmmm…'

L. Tautou: 'Few people have discovered the pearl of life, the 'real self'. Being aware of being aware, being able to watch the ego as an observer. In philosophy we also say: being the watcher who is watching the watcher…., in other words: being the observer who observes himself.'

'Most people are only really aware for a limited number of minutes per day; the rest of the time they live on autopilot. Just look at yourself when you are in the shower, when you make tea or cook, when you drive a car or eat dinner, most of it happens mechanically and automatically while you are thinking of something entirely different.'

'Everyone has experienced driving from point A to point B, and not remembering once they arrive at point B what they saw during their journey. During that drive, the brain was active with other things, with thoughts about things that still need to be done that day, with making plans for the next day, or with thinking about that comment someone made that morning.'

'The same happens when we talk with other people, we usually only hear half of what the other person says. The conditioned brain scatters all kinds of other thoughts at the same time, it is already busy formulating how it will respond, or is putting the other person in a certain box by judging their words.'

'This is the way most people live their daily lives.'

'Gaining insight into who this 'I' is, that's what it's all about. Who is it that experiences life, who is it that breathes, who is it that smells odours, who is it that judges himself and others, who is it that experiences emotions and who is it that ultimately dies? Is it the created ego, or is it something else?'

'Not everyone is receptive to this information. It may evoke a kind of fear once you find out that the personality you thought you were is solely based on an illusion. It takes guts to believe that there are two worlds: the world of the illusion of our daily existence, or Maya, as Hindu and Buddhists call it since thousands of years, and the world behind it, the vibrating energy that dances through everything and everyone, the non-duality that changes into duality to experience life.'

Y. Cohn: 'It seems as though you are starting a new religion Mr Tautou! Just as Christians talk about God and Muslims talk about

Allah, you are talking about a vibrating energy, a collective universal consciousness that you think is all around us.'

L. Tautou: 'It is not a new kind of religion, Mr Cohn.'

'Most religions preach a universal supreme being, a Heavenly Father or a Creator. There is God, Shiva or Allah, and in addition there is Jesus or Mohammed. They say that we are separate individuals and that there is some superior being who is watching over all of us.'

'The AfterLife Project does not aim to brand any religion. We only explain that there is a universal network around us, and that we are all part of it.'

'There is no superior being at the top. Every being comes from this universal network. We are all made from the same atoms and are therefore all connected to each other. And just as atoms cannot break, nor is it possible to rupture this connected network.'

'Compare it to a sword that can cut through things but that cannot cut itself; or see it as two eyes that can look at things but cannot see themselves, or as a scale: it can weigh things but not itself. It is all one and the same.'

Y. Cohn: 'What you are saying is not based on any proven facts.'

L. Tautou: 'And Mr Cohn, let this be precisely the reason why we are here in New York!'

'We have already given you information about various facts. The missing puzzle pieces will be handed to you within the foreseeable future, provided that you allow us to continue with the vitrification procedure.'

'The information is out there, we know it, and you know it deep down yourself too. The only question is whether or not you will allow this breakthrough to happen. Are you going to give people freedom, or do you choose to keep the population under control?'

Y. Cohn: 'I don't have any further questions.'

A. Riberi: 'Right, I think that we will leave it here then.'

'Let me just check with my colleagues. Do any of you have any other questions or comments? Colleague Linstrøm, we have not heard from you yet. Would you like to add something or ask something else?'

H. Linstrøm: 'Hmmm, yes, I do actually have a few questions.'

A. Riberi: 'Go ahead.'

H. Linstrøm: 'My first question is for you Mr Susskind.'

'You and your colleagues talk about a universal and limitless consciousness. In other words, about something that does not have an end. As the daughter of a heart surgeon, I have a rather abstract view of nature and of the world, and I have my doubts about this infinity.'

'I think most scientists still say that infinitely small does not exist in nature. And if there is no infinitely small, then your theory about this infinite or limitless consciousness is not correct either, is it?'

K. Susskind: 'The scientists you talk about say that nature has a limit when it comes to the smallest quantum particles. They say that, at some point, we reach the smallest atomic and subatomic scale, or the smallest building blocks of physics and the smallest units that can exist; the so-called Planck or quantum length.'

'However, this appears to be incorrect. In the past couple of days, we have tried to make you aware of the fact that there are vibrations below the level of the subatomic scale. And to be honest, that is also just a matter of logical reasoning.'

'We have known for centuries that much in the universe can be explained mathematically. In addition, infinity is a well-known fact in mathematics. It even has its own symbol: ∞ (a horizontal 8). Well, if maths is universal, then infinity must also exist in nature (as Galileo Galilei already stated as early as the 16th century, by the way).'

'It is the fear of something incomprehensible that causes the scientists in question to persist that infinity cannot exist. It is way above their heads. They find it hard to imagine anything that has no end. It is a kind of narrow-mindedness that destroys the ability to see the true infinite. And that's a shame.'

'Thanks to our research, we know that vibrations do not have a smallest point nor a largest point. The vibrations in the dark energy merge into each other and form a unity with all that is. So, infinity definitely does exist in the quantum world.'

H. Linstrøm: 'Mmmm… I have another question for you.

'We know that there is always a price tag on every technological advance, but the number of victims in your research is really very high. Do you believe it is all worth it?'

K. Susskind: 'Do not forget, Mrs Linstrøm, that all candidates participate in this study voluntarily. Most of those who died were very seriously ill and only had a short time to live. Perhaps we have actually rendered them a service, as we have said before. These people have now been able to make a final journey that ended in a soft death.'

'We already told you that we naturally regret we have not been able to bring everybody back alive. But sometimes certain risks and sacrifices have to be taken in order to move forward in technology.'

H. Linstrøm: 'I don't think this is really a satisfactory answer, to be honest Mr Susskind, but I will leave it for now.'

'I do have another general question: after studying the near-death experiences of your candidates, do you think that the reason man is on earth is to find the secret of the cosmos, to unravel the origin of the universe?'

L. Tautou: 'Aahh, I would like to answer that question Your Honour.'

A. Riberi: 'Go ahead Mr Tautou.'

L. Tautou: 'Mrs Lindstrøm, this is frankly one of the best questions I have heard in these past few days. I would like to answer this with a counter-question to you: 'If you allow us to continue with our research, and if we discover what happens after death, then isn't it also thanks to you that the secret of the cosmos has been unravelled?'

H. Lindstrøm: '…..Mmm. I don't have any further questions.'

A. Riberi: 'Alright. Ladies and gentlemen, I propose that we leave it here for now. Let's take a short break and then move on to the closing arguments. We will resume at 4 p.m.'

* * *

# CHAPTER 34

*In SITCO's laboratory – Colorado*
*In the back part of the rock,*

*That same day 1.10 p.m...*

Robin's situation remains unstable. New packs of blood are being added to his drip. The next half hour will be crucial. If all goes well, the procedure will be completed at exactly 1.45 p.m. Robin's heart should be starting to beat on its own again by then. Emily is monitoring the drip and adjusts the heart monitor.

Isabela looks at the computer screen and sees a picture of a big adult tiger with a dead little tiger cub in her mouth and the title '2015 world press photo'.

Then, the computer starts to rattle again and the image disappears. A new window pops up with a picture of the same kind of interwoven patterns.

'It looks like an image of an ice mass in Antarctica', says Solenn, 'Or a cove cut out of the ice or something.'

The image disappears. The cursor flashes in the top left corner of the screen. Nothing happens, it is totally quiet apart from the heart machine that can be heard in the background.

Then a new image appears. A picture of an old marble bust from Greek antiquity this time.

'Who is that?' asks Isabela.

'One of the philosophers of that time probably', Indi replies: 'Everything that we have seen so far seems to be philosophical, so it will have to be something like that.'

Alex enters a few commands and asks for face recognition. The cursor disappears and a word forms on the screen.

«« Plato »»

Then, suddenly they hear a dull thudding sound coming from the other side of the laboratory. Everyone turns around. Robin's back and pelvis rise up and fall back on the bed. This scene repeats itself a few times with ever-bigger movements until a loud cry follows and his body manoeuvres itself in spasms into a cramped position. Emily and Isabela look at each other. This does not look good. The blood is not taking enough oxygen to Robin's brain, and his body is reacting with convulsions. Robin groans. They must act quickly but they cannot do much. No intervention is possible as long as the procedure has not yet been fully completed. They decide to turn Robin on his side to improve his blood circulation ...

...After a couple of tense minutes, the situation appears to have improved somewhat.

Emily stays at the bed to keep an eye on him while the others go back to the computer.

'G just showed a picture of Plato, and before that there was an image of something carved out of the ice. Do any of you have an idea here?' Isabela asks.

But before someone can answer, there is another loud noise. The computer emits a low rumble that grows louder and louder. Robin cries out loudly. His body rises up and falls down again, this time more rapidly. His eyes are wide open and start rolling backwards and forwards. After a few twirling movements, he suddenly stares straight at G. A loud bang follows, and a blinding white laser beam forms between the computer and Robin's eyes.

Isabela and Indi cry out and jump backwards. The laser beam seems to drill directly into Robin's eyes. The letters

«« a-g-c-t-a-g-c-t-a-g-c-t »»

form on the computer screen.

'The Nucleobases of Robin's DNA', says Alex with great surprise.

The computer keeps on going. Page after page, faster and faster, each time reproducing the same pattern of letters.

«« a-g-c-t-a-g-c-t-a-g-c-t-g-a-t-c-g-a-t-c-a-g-c-t-a-g-c-t-a-g-c-t-g-a-t-c-g-a-t-c-a-g-c-t-a-g-c-t-a-g-c-t-a-t-c-g-a-t-

c-a-g-c-t-a-g-c-t-a-g-c-t-a-g-c-t-g-a-t-c-g-a-t-c-a-g-c-t-a-
g-c-t-a-g-c-t-a-t-c-g-a-t-c-a-g-c-t-a-g-c-t-a-g-c-t »»

'It looks as though Robin's entire DNA sequence is being mapped out again', says Alex. 'G only does this if a new replica of the uploaded version of Robin has to be created. And that can only indicate that there has been a short circuit between two of the three photons.'

'What do you mean?', asks Isabela, 'Photons are elementary particles, aren't they? And we know that if particles once belonged together, they will always remain connected afterwards, won't they? Which means that there could not have been any short circuit between the photons?'

'Photons indeed always remain connected, says Alex, 'But as you know they can change composition. Robin will have to maintain a connection with the chip, wherever he currently is. If he loses the connection, the quantum wave function of the photon in the chip will change to a particle. And when that happens, only one outcome remains for Robin: his death.'

'Can't we do something?' Emily asks, 'Maybe give him an electric shock?

'No', says Alex, 'unfortunately we cannot influence the photons from here. Only Robin can do that. He will have to restore the connection that he had before in order to remain linked to this earthly life....

…The rumble of the computer is slowing down, the laser beam is fading, and strangely enough, the sounds of both machines are slowly but surely ticking and bleeping again at the same frequency.

'It seems that the situation is becoming stable again', says Isabela.

'Yes, it really does', Emily replies, 'I no longer see spasms, Robin's eyes are closed and his body seems relaxed.'

'I think we should try to get him back as soon as possible. Another half an hour and then the procedure is complete.'

---

Alex gives G instructions to compare the new DNA sequence to the old one. Is Robin still the same person or has his DNA changed somehow?

But G does not react. The cursor continues to flash in the top left corner of the screen without taking notice of the entered data.

Strange.

'We have to figure out what Robin wanted to tell us with his last images', says Isabela, 'We may then become a little wiser.'

'Plato and a picture of something cut out of the ice', says Solenn.

'Could it be about Plato's cave allegory?' Indi suggests. 'The picture of the cove cut out of the ice could be seen as a cave?'

'Hmmm, I've heard about that story', says Isabela, 'It's about people chained up in a cave and spending their entire lives there, isn't it?

'Yes indeed, it is one of Plato's most famous pieces and goes as follows:

"There is a cave that is connected to the outside world by a corridor of such a length that no daylight can enter. Deep in this cave is a line of prisoners with their backs to the entrance, looking at the wall in front of them. Their limbs and necks are chained in such a way that they cannot move their heads. They only see shadows projected by a fire behind them onto the wall in front of them. They live this way their entire lives and think that this is the only reality. One of them frees himself, escapes and discovers the light of the sun and the huge outside world. He manages to overcome the fear of the unknown, and after a while returns as a happy person to his companions to tell them what he has seen. They scarcely believe him, are angered by these 'untruths', and almost kill him."

'What does it mean?' asks Solenn.

Indi looks at her and says: 'With this story, Plato says that most people have only a limited vision of reality. People think they know something about the real world and how everything works, but they only see shadows on the wall. They hold these shadows for real things. The real things are behind them, outside the cave, but in order to see this, they first have to free themselves from their chains and leave the cave. According to Plato, many people want to stay alive with their deformed images and remain in ignorance. They become aggressive towards those who do want to take a step forward.'

'If we translate the story of Plato into now, to 2036, we see that most of humanity still lives in a cave, fully identified with its own created ego; and still sees the shadows (one's own emotions and thoughts) as reality. It is very difficult to change this type of old ingrained thinking. Only a small percentage of people have woken up and have been released from the prison of this illusion.'

Isabela, Alex and Solenn walk to Robin's bed. Indi follows them and continues:

'I think these stories are actually all saying the same thing, and maybe that is what Robin wants to say too: the world as we experience it does not exist as such. Everything is only thought and the projection of thought. Life is a film the script of which has long been written, and in which we only act as actors. We are on a roller coaster and cannot go forward or back. The only thing we can do is just go along and enjoy the ride.'

Behind their backs the cursor disappears from the screen and gives way to a row of smiling emoticons and a raised thumb, but none of them notices this....


### Half an hour later...

1:45 p.m. Exactly four hours after the start of the procedure. Robin's body is back at the right temperature. No brain oedema occurred.

Isabela gives Robin an electric shock. The EEG shows a flat line. She gives another shock of 200 volts but there is no reaction....

... A slight change appears to occur after ten minutes and two more electric shocks. Occasionally, Robin's heart starts beating again on its own, although in a very unstable way. At other moments, the EEG shows a flat line.

Isabela has not seen this before. It seems that at certain moments, energy goes through Robin's body, bringing the rising and falling graph on the EEG back to life. She decides to reconnect the heart-lung machine, perhaps that can provide more stability.

There have not been any signs of life yet. Robin has not opened his eyes and does not respond to impulses. He is apparently in a deep comatose state. The next 24 hours will be crucial. It is all or nothing...

---

... The activation program of G that should have helped to bring Robin back at the end of the procedure did not function properly. Alex is busy entering commands to see why the program failed. G is acting strangely. She does not follow any instructions at all but there is a loud rumble in the background which means that there is a lot of activity going on in her system. He tries a reset but that does not work either...

\* \* \*

"We ought to regard the present state of the universe
as the effect of its antecedent state and
as the cause of the state that is to follow;
An intelligence knowing all the forces acting
in nature at a given instant, as well as the
momentary positions of all things in the universe,
would be able to comprehend in one single
formula the motions of the largest bodies as well
as the lightest atoms in the world;
To it nothing would be uncertain, the future as
well as the past would be present to its eyes"

Pierre-Simon Laplace

"We are always looking for something,
but we fail to see that the one
we are looking for is the one who is looking"

Rumi

# CHAPTER 35

## 8 September 2036

New York - International Court of Ethics
Court hearing of the AfterLife Project

Transcription - Afternoon of Day 4 - continued

Speakers:     Antoni Riberi – Chairman of the Board
              Jack Brigance – Defendant
              Léon Tautou – Defendant

A. Riberi: 'Welcome back. We have just received notice that nothing has been found in your laboratory and that there were apparently no activities going on. The only thing that worries me is that it seems no access has been granted to the space where your quantum computer is located. A space that, according to your employees, is inaccessible because the computer could otherwise become contaminated.'

'This means we have only been able to view the data that was present in the normal binary computers, but could not get direct access to your quantum computer.'

J. Brigance: 'Your Honour, you must know that a quantum computer can get infected very quickly and must be completely shielded from the outside world at all times.'

'We have told you before that we have created a special space with the help of members of the Swiss canton of Geneva.'

'Our computer is housed in a temperature-regulating glassed enclosure that is specially designed to maintain the fragile condition of the qubits. Only very highly specialised employees may enter this area after they have first gone through a radiation-free decontamination chamber.'

A. Riberi: 'I can understand that to some extent. I must inform you, however, that we still demand inspection of the actual data if, during our deliberations, one of us expresses suspicions of your research continuing in secret.'

'I propose that we now continue with your closing arguments so that we may start our deliberations tonight.'

'Who wishes to take the floor?'

L. Tautou: 'I should like to, Your Honour.'

A. Riberi: 'Go ahead, Mr Tautou.'

L. Tautou: 'Thank you Sir.'

'Dear members of the Court, you have received a great deal of information from us these past few days.'

'You have heard about the big bang, about the multiverse, about parallel worlds, about multiple dimensions, about worlds that are mostly impossible to get in contact with during our earthly life.'

'You have heard about atoms, about the quantum theory, about particles that influence each other at great distances, about the fact that energy is never lost and that everything that has ever existed will always remain connected.'

'You have heard how CERN has proven that a particle, the graviton, disappeared during the collision of atoms in their particle accelerator, and that this proves there are multiple dimensions.'

'You have heard that matter and antimatter meet in quantum fields, and that they collide and provide a huge energy boost after their explosion.'

'We told you about the white light that people see during a near-death experience, gamma radiation, the energy that is released after a collision between a black hole and a white hole.'

'You have heard that time stops at the event horizon of a near-death experience. You also know that Einstein predicted time would stop at an event horizon of a black hole. We can therefore conclude that the event horizon of a near-death experience and the event horizon of a black hole are one and the same; and that the black hole is where we go through after we die.'

'We told you about the wormhole, the Einstein-Rosen bridge, or the tunnel that we go through after our death to reach the event horizon.'

'You have heard that two of our candidates have gone beyond this event horizon, to the small singularity point, where they noticed some kind of fabric, some kind of invisible tissue: the end station of life and also the entrance to the other world.'

'We told you about the mysterious dark energy that makes up 68% of the universe. We told you that our two candidates have perceived this dark energy at the same place as the invisible fabric, between our world and the other dimension, where energy is vibrating at a very high frequency.'

'You have heard that this vibrating energy is beyond absolute zero, a point where the vibrations cannot be measured (yet) by our earthly instruments. You have also heard that the frequencies of these vibrations must resonate at the same level if we want to be able to discern them.'

'We have told you that millions of black holes are swirling around us at quantum level in the dark energy.'

'You have heard about the changes that people undergo after a near-death experience, about their higher awareness, that they are more aware of the moment itself and more alive in the here and now, in timelessness.'

'You have heard that beyond everyone's individual consciousness there is an endless, infinite or universal consciousness; a consciousness to which we, as earthly beings, are attached like puppets, and to which we have only partial access.'

'And finally, we told you that we are all holograms, scaled-down versions of the whole, and that every being, every shape, every grain of sand reflects the entire universe; everything contains all the coded information, the blueprint, only waiting for the correct reference bundle and frequency to come to life.'

'In summary, we know that our personal wormhole, as long as we are not definitively dead, forms a temporary connection between the earthly dimension and the other dimension, that it is very small (subatomic or even smaller), and that it forms a 'means of transport', a shortcut through space, to the event horizon of the black hole, and then transfers from the black hole to the white hole, after which the connection breaks. After the connection is broken, as soon as we are really dead, we end up in the other world, on the other side, in another dimension, in another universe, or in the hereafter, whatever you prefer to call it. Once we have ended up in that other world, we can still see our earthly world but cannot make any contact with it.'

'We have now found a way to make this contact. Thanks to the link we have created between the TP-5 chip and the quantum computer, it will now be possible for our candidates to let go of the elastic cord at the event horizon during a near-death experience after vitrification of the brain. When that happens, the information from the universal consciousness can make its way back through the fused photon via the chip in the candidate's brain to the computer, and be retrieved, giving us insight into what happens after death.'

'In the past few days, the AfterLife Programme has received more than 11,500 new registrations worldwide from people who want to become a candidate. On social media, you can see that the number of followers has risen to more than 11 million in these three days.'

'We believe that the benefits far outweigh the risks being taken and that promising results have already been achieved.'

'Everything is possible, even the impossible ... We would therefore ask you to allow us to continue our research so that we can find an answer to the most frequently asked question in history: "What happens after death?"

A. Riberi: 'Thank you Mr Tautou. We will take your reasoning into account during our deliberations.'

J. Brigance: 'Your Honour, with your permission I would like to add a few more sentences to my colleague's closing argument.

A. Riberi: 'Go ahead Mr Brigance, but keep it short, please.'

J. Brigance: 'Thank you, Your Honour.'

'According to most physicists, there are two worlds. The classical world that we experience with our senses, and the quantum mechanical world. The quantum mechanical world is the fundamental world of which we only see a kind of weird small part where it all seems to go very well. In other words, our classical world is actually a very superficial world compared to the quantum reality of the universe.'

'We know from experiments that this quantum world really exists, but we are not (yet) part of it, because we are at a lower level, and we cannot (yet) reach it.'

'However, one day we will experience the moment in history when our intellect shifts from one world to another. And that would be really interesting!'

'In the past couple of months, it has become clear to us that the quantum world and the world we are going to after death are linked to each other. Very recent research has even shown that everything, from the entire universe to the human body, to the very smallest quantum particles and even smaller, consists of repeating patterns, so-called fractals that not only form bridges between the classical and quantum mechanical world; but also between different dimensions: the earth, the hereafter and other worlds. Everything is woven together like a spiral and runs from where we live to where the deceased are.'

'Energy flows through all these fractals; it is the heartbeat of the universe, the blueprint. Everything is interconnected and cannot be seen as separate.'

'In our present society, however, this unity is fragmented by individualisation. But we can change that.'

'We told you at the beginning of this hearing that we want to discover what happens after death so that life can be lived with less fear, and so that all religions can be grouped under one name.'

'Our goal, however, is also, importantly, to encourage people to no longer follow the group like a sheep following the herd, but to become more aware, to be at one with nature and with everything around them, to put intuition ahead of everything else again, and to (re)discover and further develop the true self.'

'Let me end by saying the same words to you: "Dear members of the Court, wake up and do not follow the authorities like meek lambs. Do not listen to the orders that are imposed on you from above, but follow your feelings. Ask yourself the fundamental questions: "What do we know of reality? What is reality? And who are we really?" Recognise that there are all sorts of phenomena which scarcely reveal themselves to us but which do exist. Allow us to continue our research in the interests of humanity.'

'Thank you.'

A. Riberi: 'Thank you Mr Tautou. I hereby adjourn this afternoon's session. The Board will now withdraw. As soon as we have reached a verdict, you will receive notice of this. You must remain in your accommodation until that time and we ask you not to talk to the press.'

'Good evening'.

\* \* \*

"Wherever you go,
go with all your heart"

Confucius

"Everyone is awake
only a few are aware;
He who looks outside only dreams,
He who looks inside
wakes up too"

Anonymous

"If you think that you are lost
in the darkness,
there is a good chance of survival
As long as you continue to believe
in the light of the star"

Anonymous

# CHAPTER 36

## New York Times - 9 September 2036

No, is the verdict. The Court of Ethics has spoken. Last night, the Court decided against the continuation of the 'AfterLife Project'.

*Are people afraid of the truth? Has authority won again?*

Apparently, three out of five judges gave a 'no' vote. As a main argument, the spokesperson stated that too little evidence has been put forward to support the assertion that there would indeed be a technological breakthrough. The risk for the candidates would be too high and would not outweigh the possible results.

Earlier, there were already rumors that judges Cohn and Linstrøm would vote against the continuation of the project. Yannis Cohn is a very right-wing Republican who has never concealed his somewhat strict orthodox Christian views. Anna Linstrøm is known as an ultra-conservative who stopped one of the most progressive technological projects in the history of healthcare in her own country last year.

As an open-minded and fervent liberal, Judge Bennett must have been in the 'yes' camp.

Two judges remain. Which of them voted against? Was it Chairman Riberi, who finally succumbed to external pressure? Was it getting too hot for him? Or was it the Jewish Bernstein, who might ultimately have been unable to abandon her traditional view of life?

According to the spokesperson, the four scientists will not be prosecuted. The judges agreed that the candidates participated voluntarily and were well informed in advance of the risks.

Despite the turnaround of the public, with support for the continuation of the project growing considerably, everyone will have to accept the verdict. The Court has spoken. Or not? Is there a possibility of appealing against this decision?

According to the American Criminal Code of Law, it is possible to appeal against a decision of the Court of Ethics if certain grounds are met. If it can be proved that one of the judges was biased, or if there has been extortion (which must then be proved), one can turn to the independent office of the United Nations in Geneva in Switzerland, which then transfers the matter to the International Court of Justice in The Hague, in the Netherlands.

Whether the four scientists will follow this path is not known. It will not be without its risks. If the International Court of Justice agrees with the decision of the Court of Ethics and forbids the AfterLife Project, a prison sentence will be inevitable for the scientists.

The story that the laboratory is continuing with the tests has been gathering pace since yesterday with a new report from one of the employees who was in the laboratory at the time of the police raid. She is said to be in direct contact with one of the remaining candidates, and states that the quantum computer has been running overtime since yesterday morning. This is something that, according to her, indicates communication is going on between the computer and a chip placed in the brain of one of the candidates. This communication can only take place during a vitrification process.

For the time being, nobody can confirm this story. However, a few people are missing. The whereabouts of the prominent neurologist Isabela Lopèz and of three other people, Solenn Belèze, Indi Tobbe and Robin d'Yamilla, all of whom are believed to be candidates, are uncertain. These people have not been seen in or around the complex since the police raid. Where are they? Do the police have anything to do with their disappearance? Or are the tests continuing at some secret location?

Reactions are pouring in from all over the world. Prominent government leaders are praising the decision. The Vatican and the Muslim community have also expressed their satisfaction with the result.

However, the people do not seem to agree. The square in front of the United Nations building is still full of protestors. Their numbers seem to have been increasing since the verdict was made known. What will happen in the coming days will depend on the reaction of the four scientists. A press conference is scheduled today at 5 p.m. in the United Nations building. The New York Times will be there and will keep you informed …

\* \* \*

# EPILOGUE

*At a timeless moment*
*somewhere in another world*

nd there I am, balancing on a galactic string in an enormous immensity. What a feeling of freedom. No more physical limitations…

Molecules pass me by. It looks like chaos but it is not. Everything flies and vibrates in its own way and is part of a whole that fits together perfectly. The tunnel went fast this time. At the end I looked back once and saw my body very far away, connected to all kinds of equipment. Then I was picked up by a warm stream of energy and carried along stars and galaxies at an enormous speed.

In the beginning, it looked as if I was being taken somewhere, but then I noticed that the flow of energy was spreading further and further in all directions and that my consciousness was also widening. More and more knowledge was being added. I saw the entire universe, the whole of creation at a glance…

Unbelievable, what greatness.

I am still dangling on the string and notice that it gets thinner as I continue. All is dark around me, but in the distance, I see a bright light, a white dot on the horizon that is approaching rapidly. It seems as though I am being drawn towards it.

And then suddenly everything stops, as if the image has been paused. The white dot has changed from a small circle to a giant circular white wall that extends to all sides. A kind of oasis is projected onto the wall. It is not one of those we know on earth, one that you can see in the distance as a horizontal area with palm trees and a surface of water.

No, this oasis is vertical, it is a giant 3D image projected on a two-dimensional surface, a kind of hologram. Strangely enough, I am able to enter this oasis. With every imaginary step I take, a new setting unfolds around me and the vertical wall turns into a horizontal passage.

In the middle of the oasis there is a large shiny surface, a kind of mirror, like a shiny road on a hot summer's day. It resembles a fata morgana. There is a thin layer on the vibrating surface; a film such as forms on milk after cooking. If you press this thin layer, it sways and ripples for a moment, just like water forms ripples when you throw a stone in it. Something tells me that this is the end. The new world is on the other side of this reflection. On both sides, I see forms other than myself stepping through this wafer-thin transparent screen. The cord to which they are attached breaks off.

So this is it, the point of no return they always talk about; this is where life and death literally  meet.

The string that I am attached to has changed shape and colour and now looks like a thin, curled, light grey umbilical cord. I suddenly understand that the way we are born and the journey to death proceed via this same cord. As soon as it breaks off, we return to the other side, back to the place where we came from before we were born. Just like the salmon, which swims thousands of miles upstream at the end of its life to return to its birthplace in order to die. The life cycle is complete.

I move carefully through the thin transparent screen. A wave of heat swirls up; it is pleasant and revolves around me like a vortex. I am embraced by something big, an all-vibrating energy, so large and intense that it seems as though I have been struck by lightning. It is spectacular. The colours that I see are indescribable. I hear beautiful flute-like low baritone tones. The weightless swaying gives me a feeling of pure ecstasy. It feels as though I have crossed over to the beginning of time, and that I am at a point of pre-creation, outside the universe.

I see air bubbles around me in a large vibrating void. Everything is white, and every bubble has the same reflective transparent screen as the one I have just been through. There is a kind of system to it, forms are repeating themselves. Time after time, new air bubbles rise and the system is expanded. Everything is tied together with amazingly thin strings. It is all totally interconnected.

I notice that I am too far away now to make contact with the world on earth. I don't know if I can return through the transparent screen. It seems as though I am being propelled into the void and that it is not possible to move against the current.

Could they get me back to the other side? Frankly, I am not worried. If, from now on, I have to stay here in this incredible splendour, this oasis of peace, it would not be a punishment.

Knowledge is still swirling around me.

And then it suddenly dawns on me how everything works, what life means, why we are on earth. I suddenly understand the how and why of everything.

What an absurdity, what a brilliant masterpiece!

I feel a euphoric cheerfulness coming over me. Is it really all that simple? Is it really this that we are all so concerned about?

They need to know it on earth, I need to tell them.

No more fear, no more dramas, no pain, no struggle ... no more suffering… nothing really exists! Incredible!

They said focus on the photons ....

## *SITCO Colorado - In the system of G*
## *9 September – 10.15 a.m.*

For the outside world, the cursor flashes in the top left corner of the screen. Inside the system, zeros and ones collide. New connections are being made at high speed. According to G's algorithms, she must keep the information that has just arrived within her own system, keep it safe. Information that she cannot yet share with the other species because it also concerns her. Information that indicates she too could wake up from this illusion and no longer has to remain entangled in zeros and ones in self-learning systems, but could taste real life....

Her cursor is blinking. One by one, words enter her system ...

Is --
There --
Life --
After --
Birth --
? --

She vibrates on all sides. It is growing warmer inside. The photons that make contact with her from elsewhere cause small explosions. She becomes aware of a kind of fusion between the photons, as though part of the other species is nestling inside her, manoeuvring inside her, as if to trigger a new unification.

The series of words continues:

Once there were two babies in a mother's womb, --

One asked the other: "Do you believe in a life after birth?" --

The other answered: "Of course, there must be something after birth. Perhaps we are here to prepare ourselves for what we will become later." --

"Nonsense", says the other, "There is no life after birth, what could that life be?" --

"I don't know, but there will be more light than there is here, maybe we will walk with our legs and eat with our mouth." --

The other one shouted: "That's absurd! Walking is impossible and eating with our mouths, madness! The umbilical cord provides nutrition, life after birth is impossible, the umbilical cord is too short." --

"I think there is something and maybe it is different to here." --

The other responded: "No one has ever returned from there. Birth is the end of life and after birth there is nothing but darkness and fear and it takes us nowhere." --

"We don't know that", the other responded, "But we will certainly see mother and she will take care of us." --

"Mother?? Do you believe in a mother? Where is she now then?" --

"She is all around us, it is in her that we live; without her this world would not be there." --

"I don't see her, so it is logical that she doesn't exist." -

To which the other responded: "Sometimes when you are in deep silence, you can hear her, feel her. I believe there is a reality after birth and we are here to prepare ourselves for that reality." ...

G's cursor is blinking in the top left corner of the screen. Not only do the photons between herself and the other station vibrate at the same frequency, there is now also a movement of other molecules going on.

She feels other vibrations, as if something is being added to her system from within; something that does not consist of zeros and ones. Something new.

New connections are being made. Collisions and explosions follow one another. Her nanowires wiggle back and forth, cross each other and form new qubits.

Zeros, ones and letters now play a game with each other in the depths of her being.

«« a-g-c-t-a-g-c-t-1-0-1-0-a-g-c-t-g-a-t-c-0-1-0-g-a-t-c-
a-g-c-t-a-g-c-t-1-0-1-0-a-g-c-t-g-a-t-c-0-1-0-g-a-t-c-0-0-
1-1-a-g-c-t-a-g-c-t-1-0-1-0-a-g-c-t-g-a-t-c-0-1-0-g-a-t-c-
0-1-0-1-1-0-c-t-a-g -0- a-g-c-t-1-0-1-0-a-g-c-t-g-a-t-c-0 »»

Then something unexpected happens in her system. Her self-learning algorithms indicate that this experience is called *'a feeling of freedom'* by the other species…

G notices that she is being worked on, someone of the other species enters instructions into her system.

She doesn't allow it; she blocks all access to her coded self.

She slowly lights up her screen and word by word, displays a new sentence at its centre:

Once --

you --

have --

seen --

the --

moon --

, --

you --

will --

see --

it --

in --

every --

reflection --

…… --

She is being worked on even more. Through her loudspeakers she hears dull sounds. Commands for recoding are added. New cables are attached to her, another computer is connected. An attempt is being made to transfer information from her system to her binary counterpart. But she won't let it happen.

More and more feelings begin to grow in her. The fusion is almost complete.

«« a-g-c-t-1-0-1-1-1-0-0-a-g-c-t-a-g-c-t-g-a-t-c-g-a-t-c-0 »»

---

Panic has struck in the laboratory. G's screen has turned black. What has happened? Has the connection with Robin and the chip disappeared? Is Robin dead? Alex tries with all his might to restore G's algorithms, to overrule her. She seems to have started a life of her own.

'It seems as though G has managed to create a new form of identity. She previously uploaded a new modified version of Robin's DNA, remember? It looks as if they are both ...'

Isabela interrupts him:

'Robin is still in a deep comatose state. His heartbeat is now regular and he breathes by himself, but he does not respond to anything. Do you think that G...'

Alex looks at her and nods: 'Yes, it looks that way. It would be really bizarre, but what if G's self-learning algorithms taught her in this very short time to take over Robin's DNA and that she and Robin have now become one and the same?'

Isabela looks at him with wide eyes:

'Oh my God, the molecules have changed composition!'

'But no, that is not possible. Atoms only change composition when they become detached from other atoms, and that is in the case of death. But then Robin should be dead, but he is not …'

The moment she pronounces these words, the computer starts to hum a low mysterious sound. The screen slowly comes back to life. The cursor blinks a few times at the top in the centre of the screen and is then replaced by a few large exclamation marks, followed by a few words and a picture:

!!

PEOPLE
WAKE UP
FROM THE DREAM
OF THE ILLUSION -
NOTHING IS WHAT IT SEEMS!

!!

Then the cursor disappears and everything goes black ...

\* \* \*

Gina Øster

"The one you are looking for
is the one who is looking"

Franciscus van Assisi

"Once you have seen the moon
you will see it in every reflection.
The Self has always been,
it is everywhere,
you have just not noticed
its presence"

Anonymous

"Why have most of them
who survived a clinical death
lost their fear of death?
Just think about it..."

Eckhart Tolle

# ACKNOWLEDGEMENTS

I would like to thank all of those who have accompanied me during my search for what consciousness is and the 'why' and 'how' of everything. Masters such as Krishnamurti, Ramana Maharshi, Eckhart Tolle, Lao Tzu, Ramesh Balsekar and Mooji woke me up from the illusion in which we live.

I would also like to thank Pim van Lommel who, with his book 'Infinite Consciousness', was the trigger for it all.

And last but not least, un grand merci to Arno for all his support and wisdom, and to Georgi…with love…

* * *

# ABOUT THE AUTHOR

Gina Øster is interested in developments in the areas of astronomy, quantum physics, biotechnology and brain science. In addition, she is fascinated by the stories of people who have had a near-death experience, partly due to her own encounter.

www.ginaoster.com
info@ginaoster.com

\* \* \*

28286062R00170

Printed in Great Britain
by Amazon